The Thales:

Days to Launch

Thomas A. Fowler

Copyright © 2019 by Thomas A. Fowler / Nerdy Things Publishing, LLC.

All rights reserved.
Published by Nerdy Things Publishing.
NerdyThingsPublishing.com

Paperback ISBN 978-0-9973499-7-9

Ebook ISBN 978-0-9973499-8-6

THE THALES: DAYS TO LAUNCH

A NOVELLA

THOMAS A. FOWLER

NERDY THINGS PUBLISHING

Jason White and Donnie Harmon tried to keep steady on a rocking boat, waiting to see if they could change the world. The open air blew through the captain's deck of the nine-meter-long exploratory boat. The duo hovered over a control panel with two monitors, showing the readings of the small, unmanned submersible they'd deployed from the boat pouring in as Donnie navigated the bottom of the Pacific Ocean. The right monitor read the depth, coordinates, and speed of the ocean current. The left showed the front camera of the submersible. The two lights on the main hull of the vessel shone on a pitch-black surface. Specks of debris and sediment floated around, illuminated by the spotlights.

"What are we at?" Donnie asked, concentrating on navigating the submersible. He held both sticks lightly, adjusting movement in gentle motions. His hands were flexible, still nimble even though he was in his forties. He sported a strong five o'clock shadow, not far from becoming a beard with some salt mixed in with the pepper. His hair, although balding, didn't reflect the same; still a dark brown, with eyes to match.

"9.15 meters per second," Jason read from the right monitor. His fingers tapped the screen, his hands weathered from years of hard labor before becoming an analyst. The wrinkles on his skin, and around his eyes, were appropriate for a man just turning fifty. His pale blue eyes popped with color against his light, grey hair styled in a neat pompadour.

The boat rocked again. As the tides increased during the sunset, waves splashed against the silver boat, some of the impact going over the rails. Jason looked out to the west, gauging how much time they had left to run the submersible. They'd wait for the last ray of sunlight before calling it a day. Pete, their captain, kept the boat as steady as he could to allow Donnie to drive the submersible.

"How far are we from the canyon?" Donnie asked.

"Looks like we are about nine thousand meters north, plenty to go still," he replied. "We've got just under eight thousand before we'll reach the zone we can't build. Depth variances are about the same unless you want to venture further west – gets real deep once we hit the drop off."

"Okay, I think we have to go further south. We've broken single digit speeds only once, it's just not here," Donnie said.

Jason pulled up the bathymetry data for the region on his laptop. Putting it next to the controls, the map displayed depths and readings on ridges, canyons, and the varying changes to the bottom of the Pacific Ocean. He rubbed his eyes before putting on reading glasses. His eyes showed how much he'd worked to gain everything in his career; his thin frame built from years of exhaustion.

Donnie put the submersible into a hover mode, and a cloud of sand kicked up as it stopped, sitting still in the water. With how slow the current speeds were, it required minimal force, which wasn't something either of them wanted to see happen. They needed a strong current to place thousands of turbines for their renewable energy project, that would transmit power to the west coast. Until they found a suitable location, they couldn't get funding for their next stage.

On the bathymetric map, they surveyed the area. A circular blip emanated northwest of Humboldt Bay in California, indicating their position. Far offshore, the map had varying shades of blue getting darker the further the map went west, showing the increase in depth. There were a series of red marks along the edge where the third darkest shade met the fourth, indicating a depth between seven hundred and fifty meters and one thousand. Once the map hit the fourth darkest shade, the water was at least one thousand meters deep. There were thirteen red marks north of their location where they had gauged the current's power, only to get lackluster results. Only three marks were left to the south they hadn't tried.

"What happens if none of those work?" Donnie asked.

"Then we'll have to survey south of Eel Canyon," Jason replied.

"But then we can't depart from Humboldt Bay – not to mention we're getting extreme depths with less distance from the shore. The canyons and reefs down there will present all new problems," Donnie said.

Jason tapped the space on his laptop near the touchpad. He scratched his scalp, hair moving around as he dug in with his fingers. "Yup, it's a whole new set of problems. Well, we're too far up to get there today. Hey, Pete, do you mind retrieving the sub? We won't make those other three today."

"I can navigate in the dark if you want to push," Pete said, taking Donnie's seat and grabbing the submersible controls.

"No, don't worry about it, we've got until the end of the week," Jason said. "Plus, this way you can see your kids before calling it a night."

"Sure, just wanted to give the option," Pete said.

"Appreciate it." Jason sighed. "Who's making the call to Ronald McArnold?"

Donnie brought up a fist. Jason did the same. After three pumps, they shot. Donnie threw rock, Jason scissors.

"You always start with scissors, you're too predictable," Donnie smiled.

The second was a tie, both with paper. Third went to Jason when he tried scissors again, banking on Donnie varying his strategies too much.

"Now who's predictable?" Jason taunted him.

They slammed their fists against open palms three times, then shot. Jason got him again by showing paper.

"Damn it!" Donnie cursed. "Come on. He never yells at you, you're 'the golden child.'"

"How am I 'the golden child?'" he asked. "I'm fifty, and older than you."

Donnie pulled up his cell phone to call Ronald Arndt, the board executive and their point of contact. A sincere, but insistent man, Donnie and Jason's increasing frustration with his constant need for updates resulted in them nicknaming him "Ronald McArnold." It was a nickname shared in conversation by those two, they didn't dare use it with others or put it in an email. It was a way for them to vent amongst themselves. "Hey, Ronald McArnold is pushing sixty. 'Golden Prodigy' then, how's that?"

"Sure," Jason said. "I'm grabbing a drink, need anything?"

Donnie raised his water bottle, shaking it to indicate he had plenty still. "Hi, Ronald? Yes, it's Donnie Harmon, how are you?"

"Doing okay, how about you two? Good news today?" Ronald asked.

"Well, not exactly great news on our end. We surveyed five sites today, and numbers still aren't coming back where we'd like," Donnie replied.

For several minutes, Donnie remained quiet, letting Ronald get it out of his system. The executive was never unprofessional, but he was also quick to bring up project scopes and expectations from the board every time they reported back to tell him they didn't have an appropriate site for the station yet. Once he was done venting, Donnie chimed back in.

"We have three sites to inspect tomorrow. We'll start closest to Eel Canyon, it borders on the safety zone we were given, but if they push back, we've got the paper trail saying as long as it's one thousand meters' distance from the canyon, we can build there. If that doesn't work, we'll work our way north to the other two," Donnie said.

"You realize what's at stake if one of these three sites won't work, right?" Ronald asked. "Senators McCreary and Fox are asking for updates constantly. The west coast of America is depending on this station being built."

"I do," Donnie replied. "But if those don't work, we can go with our contingency of surveying south of the canyon, and our third plan is to choose our highest speed and build there, with the understanding the station will generate less energy."

"What's our goal?" Ronald asked.

"We're trying to find a spot with speeds of twenty centimeters per second, that'll maximize the turbines we've designed to generate enough energy to power the entire west coast," Donnie said.

"What's the highest speed we've clocked at the sites you've visited so far?" Ronald asked.

Donnie looked over the data on the right monitor. He knew the answer but checked it one more time to see if a magically higher number popped up somewhere. "Twelve."

"So, if one of those three sites doesn't work, then we're on the hook for three more months of surveying, delaying this again. That, or our second option is to build at a spot where we'll have a facility delivering only sixty percent of its capacity," Ronald said.

"Speeds around twenty centimeters per second have been recorded, some at twenty-five, even thirty. Unfortunately, we're discovering those are occurring in more uneven terrain where we won't be able to put anywhere close to eight thousand turbines and a transmission station. The higher speeds cause an increase in corrosion, creating ridges and canals that are not buildable sites."

The phone was silent. Donnie started talking a couple times, taking in a breath, then stopping before he spoke, waiting for Ronald to respond. "Ronald?"

"Yup, still here," Ronald said. "Let's find a site tomorrow that works, okay?"

"Okay," Donnie replied. "And we can always look at sites deeper than a thousand meters, too, it'll just add significantly to construction costs. The ship we have is only fitted to deliver materials to nine hundred and fifty meters. We've got options."

"Options that cost us more money and time," Ronald responded. "Call me tomorrow to tell me one of those three sites will work."

"We'll try," Donnie said.

"I don't want to hear 'try,' find me a site tomorrow, okay?" Ronald said.

Donnie paused, knowing he couldn't make that guarantee. He tried to think of a response. "We'll... call you tomorrow."

He hung up the phone before Ronald could respond. A nervous laugh escaped him.

Jason tapped Pete's shoulders. "Hey Pete, I can take over. Do you mind getting us ready to head in once we get the submersible on board?"

"Sure thing." Pete headed for the wheel of the nine-meter-long boat. The gray and green lines of paint on the otherwise silver hull started from the pointed bow, ending at the wide stern where the submersible was housed within a welded metal framework, along with a winch for raising and lowering it from the boat.

Donald sat next to Jason, sighing while putting his head in his hands. "Can we meet first thing tomorrow? Decide which area we want to go after first?" Donnie asked. "I'm a little worried for our job security if tomorrow doesn't pan out."

"You think so?" Jason asked, steering the submersible toward the surface.

"Right now, unless one of those spots pulls through tomorrow, the three options we have for Ron are build deeper, survey a whole new area, or capture forty percent less energy than what we expected." Donnie waved his three fingers about. "Either way, we're delaying the project by at least three months and costing millions of dollars more, either in upfront construction costs, lost time, or return on investment. You think the board is going to say okay without some heads rolling?"

"Shit," Jason said. "You're right. Does the bistro work?"

"I know it's not as fancy, but can we do Sun Bay Café? They open earlier," Donnie replied.

"Fine, let's load up on grease and fat before we head out to sea," Jason said.

The submersible breached the surface, the water splashing against the boat as it rose above the ocean. Pete, Jason, and Donnie worked together to connect the winch hook and get the submersible on the boat.

✳✳✳

The next day didn't go much better. They'd tested all three sites, and the best reading they had was fourteen centimeters per second.

"I mean, it's seventy percent," Jason said. "That's not bad."

"No, but long-term we could gather so much more energy. If we just had more time, I know we could find the right spot with enough force behind the current to make this work," Donnie said. "I mean, it pushes eleven million cubic meters of water per second around – surely some of it has to be moving at twenty measly centimeters per second, with a flat bed of rock somewhere in this area."

"Well, maybe that's the problem, it's pushing so much there are only select spots where it has enough force," Jason responded.

"Exactly, where there's a massive river creating Eel Canyon, it's because it's pouring out so we'd disrupt an entire ecosystem, or around ridges where we can't build because it's carving underwater mountains from all the force." Donnie stopped.

"What?" Jason asked.

Donnie grabbed the bathymetric map, looking at depths and the shapes of rock formations in their sweet spot between five hundred and one thousand meters. He noticed two elongated areas leading toward a steep drop off, going from over eight hundred meters to twelve hundred and deeper. In between the elongated stretches of rock were deep caverns.

"Hey, how many square meters for the build?" Donnie asked.

"Give me a second." Jason pulled up an email of the latest designs. He handed his phone with the plans over to Donnie.

The two calculated the space it'd take to fit the transmission station and all of the turbines.

"How many turbines were allocated to power the station and auxiliary?" Donnie asked.

"Nine hundred and fifty. Another seven thousand are going straight to the shore," Jason replied.

"Okay, but that was excessive. We only needed fifteen to power the station. The rest is backup either for us or a damaged grid or transmission cable. If we ditch a few rows, get it down to seven hundred and fifty, something like that, we can make the room. It'll be tight, but it's there," Donnie said.

"Why is that spot so special?" Jason asked.

"Look, you have the main rock bed here on the east, it should go out a lot farther. Instead you've got these two peninsulas headed to the northwest – those didn't happen by accident. Formations like that are carved." Donnie tapped the map.

"Carved by force, by sediment. By thousands of years of constant pressure that is more intense than the rest of the area." Jason pounded his fist against the table. "Pete, you up for one more?"

"I like you guys, I don't want you to get fired. This gig pays too much," Pete replied. "Where we headed?"

"Give me a minute to get you exacts, for now north-northwest!"

As they made their way, Donnie sat near the bow, coffee from the café in hand. It'd gone cold hours ago, but he liked holding it. It felt like a familiar day back at the Maritimus Energy offices before the field surveys began.

As Pete steered the boat, Jason joined Donnie up front. "You sure you want to try this?"

"Yeah, it'd be a tight fit, those turbines are going to be right up against that ridgeline. But what do we have to lose, really?"

Jason's phone vibrated. He didn't even look at it or retrieve it from his hoodie pocket.

"Is Ronnie McArnold trying you now?" Donnie asked.

"Probably, not going to look at it." Jason shook his head. "No sense in answering right now. We'll wait until we have something to say."

The sun bounced off the waves, the setting sun reflecting in the moving water. Jason and Donnie worked on preparing the submersible as they got near. Jason grabbed an air tank with a valve.

"How much are you shooting?" Donnie asked.

"Five psi," Jason asked.

"Looking at 34.47 kilopascal then." Donnie used his phone to convert the numbers. "That equals out to 3.515 meters of water."

Jason pointed the nozzle at apparatus that looked like a fan at the bottom of the small, unmanned submersible. "Ready?"

"Almost." Donnie doodled his finger on the touchpad of his laptop to wake it up. "Go."

Jason fired the nozzle, expelling compressed air into the fan. The blades spun within the small container.

"3.502." Donnie looked down at the fan. He blinked repeatedly as the air dried his eyes. He returned to the laptop. "3.51"

The compressed air continued. Jason moved the nozzle angle slightly, adjusting to see if the numbers changed.

"We're staying within 3.5 and 3.513 as you move it," Donnie said.

"Close enough?" Jason asked.

"Close enough to know the range we're dealing with. Plus, by the time the sub gets down there we're going to be losing daylight," Donnie replied.

Jason stopped the compressed air. He coiled the nozzle and hose around the tank to put it away.

"All right," Pete said. "We're here. 40.77 by -124.70."

"Thank you, sir," Jason said. "Let's drop it."

Pete stopped the boat. He pulled the winch handles to raise the submersible off the platform. The two-meter-long and one-meter-wide sub rocked a bit as the chain tightened. Jason and Donnie held either side to stabilize it. Pete navigated the winch to the portside. Jason and Donnie walked with the sub, keeping it from rocking, letting go as it moved over the edge of the boat.

Lowered into the water, the ocean jostled the sub around a bit. Donnie leaned over the edge of the boat. Jason held Donnie's belt on the back of his pants to keep him from falling over. Donnie's face went red from the inverted pressure. He reached for the hook on the winch connected to the sub and squeezed it, pulling it through the loop. The submersible splashed into the water.

"Got it," Donnie said.

Jason tugged at Donnie's belt, lurching him back over the edge. They settled in on the console and activated the monitors, waiting for the sub to dive to eight hundred meters. Eating peanut butter and jelly sandwiches during the dive, they talked about what to do if this last-ditch effort failed. Forty minutes into the dive, Ronald called them again. Jason decided to answer this time.

"Hi, Ronald. How are you?" he asked.

Donnie could only hear murmuring on the other side of the phone. He sat watching the submersible front camera. At this stage, the water was pitch black, the usual floating specks moving around in the water as the submersible made its way to the ocean bottom.

"Yup, we tried the three sites we identified. Better results on one. We're looking into one last site – it'd be a tight fit, but we can accommodate," Jason said.

On the right monitor, Donnie saw the submersible had reached seven hundred and fifty meters. He pointed at the monitor, grabbing Jason's attention, mouthing "almost there" while indicating the readout. Jason gave a thumbs up.

"I understand," Jason said to Ronald. "Yes. Yes, I understand, Ronald. I know we haven't found the results we wanted. It's… yes… it's… Ronald? It's why we're trying this site. The rock formations near it indicate small canyons nearby, we think that the current is stronger and carved those spaces. Well, they're more gorges than canyons."

Donnie couldn't understand what Ronald said in response. But he could hear the tone. Donnie's intuition was right. Ronald sounded infuriated. This was it. This was their chance; otherwise, he'd have to fire them as a display of dominance. He wouldn't be able to approach the board asking for more time and money without saying, "the problem has been dealt with."

The monitor read seven hundred and eighty-eight meters. Donnie slowed the descent. They'd never surveyed the area so even though the bathymetric data showed they had almost another hundred meters to the bottom, he wouldn't risk lowering the sub into a rocky cliffside by accident. He couldn't imagine how bad the call would be to tell him they not only failed to retrieve any data from the new potential site, but also wrecked the submersible with customized testing equipment that was worth more than his salary.

"Ronald, we're doing the best we can with what we're learning. It's why we did these surveys. We did find a site that has the potential for seventy percent capacity in terms of current speed. That's one more than we had yesterday, so additional surveying can only help us." Jason paused to wait for Ronald to stop ranting. "Ronald? Hey, Ronald? We're almost to our depth on testing the new site. Yes… I hear you. I get it."

The submersible passed eight hundred meters with nothing in sight. Donnie cycled through the front and back cameras, but only saw dark ocean. He swapped to the bottom. The spotlights on the sub would shine there first so they could at least see the bottom as it approached.

Jason rolled his hand around in circles, impatiently waiting for Ronald to finish his rant. "I understand, Ronald. I do… Ronald, trust me I do… of course, we understand the importance of reaching our capacity. I also know how this project is on track to exceed budget if we don't find a site soon. We're aware. Like I sai… like I said, we're doing what we can, with what we have available. Okay?"

At eight hundred and twenty-five meters they still hadn't reached ocean bottom.

"Ronald, I hear your concerns. We're going to check this site and get back to you, okay?" Jason said. "I don't know when we'll be in touch. We have to survey the area to make sure there's a large enough space for the transmission station. The bathymetric data can only tell us so much. We know more about the surface of the moon than we do about the bottom of the ocean. We also need to check the area to make sure we're not disrupting any sedimentary flows or reefs. We're trying to harvest energy from an incredibly powerful, but remarkably fragile, ecosystem."

Jason pulled the cell phone away, covering the mouthpiece as he took in a deep breath, sighing as he exhaled to vent his frustration.

Donnie smiled and laughed a little. "We're at eight hundred and forty-five meters, still no bottom. Keep talking with him, if you'd like."

Jason raised his middle finger and returned to the call. "Hey Ronald. Ronald? Ronald? We're at the bottom so I'm going to let you go."

Donnie whispered, "We've still got a way to go."

Jason shook his head, mouthing "shut up" to Donnie. "Yup, so it's time for us to do our job. Let us survey this spot, we'll talk in the morning. We're likely going to be here well into the night."

Donnie noticed the readout on the monitor jumped. The depth increased at a faster rate. They were at eight hundred and fifty-nine meters, dropping nearly fifteen meters in less than a minute. "Whoa."

"Okay, Ronald. Yup. Got it," Jason said. "Talk to you tomorrow."

Jason stopped talking and hung up, giving no concern to Ronald still talking. "Jesus!" He leaned forward to look at the monitor, taking notice of Donnie's face.

"What's going on?" Jason asked.

"Dive rate is way too fast," Donnie pulled up on the controls. It continued to dive, now at eight hundred and ninety-one meters. "I can't get it to slow down."

"Wait, I thought the shelf was around the high eight hundreds," Jason said.

"It is. We should at least be able to see the bottom, if not hit the damned thing," Donnie said. "We just exceeded nine hundred."

"Still going?" Jason asked.

"Yeah, still descending and not responding. Engines aren't pushing hard enough to resist what's pushing it," Donnie replied.

After a few more minutes, they surpassed one thousand meters depth. The bottom finally came into view of the camera.

"Damn it," Donnie said. "It's deeper than we thought."

"Shit," Jason looked at the camera feed. "We can't go over one thousand, can we?"

"Not unless we get a new ship for construction, or retrofit it with additional cabling," Donnie replied.

"Wait, pan the sub to the left," Jason said. "Bring up all the monitors, too."

Donnie pushed a button, so the left monitor stopped showing just the bottom camera. The top, front, and back cameras shared the screen's four corners along with the bottom. As the sub turned, rocks were on either side of the front and back.

"We're not on the flat portion," Jason said. "We're in one of the gorges. Look at that incline."

"How'd we get there?" Donnie asked.

"You lost control when? Around eight hundred and fifty meters?" Jason asked.

Donnie nodded.

"What if the water pushed it into the gorge?" Jason asked.

"Because it was so damned forceful." Donnie slapped Jason's shoulders.

He turned the sub further, facing the front of the sub toward the inlet of the gorge. Facing the current directly, he turned on the signaling for the current monitor. It took a moment for the readout to arrive and transmit.

"Eighteen meters per second and it just started," Donnie said. "Fan's still increasing. Twenty-one… Twenty-six… Thirty-one! We're at thirty-one meters per second. 31.2, 31.1, 31.25."

The two watched the number, holding for a moment to make sure it was true.

"We're holding steady around thirty-one meters per fucking second!" Donnie shouted.

"Yes! Okay," Jason said. "Now, we have to get above the gorge, check the flatter area where the station would rest. See if that's the case or if it's slower up there."

Donnie activated the bottom motors to get above it all. "It must be, otherwise this gorge would be a much wider canyon."

They raised the sub, passing a small school of jellyfish. The edges of the gorge got wider the higher they rose. Donnie kept it close to the edge so they could see when they'd reached the top. A curve sloped toward a flat terrain.

"All right, we're here. Eight hundred and seventy-five meters. Reading of twenty-six meters per second," Donnie said. "Man, that's a huge drop once we got above that downward swell."

"We're still well above range though," Jason said.

"It's going to drop fast the further we go," Donnie replied.

"We don't know for sure – head in, take a look," Jason said.

The area had a few curves and small ridges here and there. However, the bed of rock remained relatively flat.

"Can you hold there? Getting the exact coordinates." Jason jotted the latitude and longitude down. "Okay, keep going toward that big inclining ridge, that's how far we have for width on the build."

Donnie moved the sub forward. "Already down to twenty-four meters per second after heading in three meters."

"It'll hold," Jason said.

"Twenty-three," Donnie said.

They had a long way to the ridge on the other side. It was in view of the front camera, but appeared as a vague silhouette against more darkness at the ocean bottom.

"Twenty-two." Donnie kept piloting the sub toward the ridge.

"We just passed with enough space for one row of turbines, so at least one row is at capacity," Jason said. "We need fifty-four meters of space for the station."

"Down to twenty-one," Donnie said.

The drone moved along the shelf: no apparent reef growth, a few fish. Nothing to hinder them from building there.

"Twenty point five." Donnie shook his head.

"We just need another twenty meters for the second row of turbines," Jason said. "It'll hold."

"Twenty point seven five," Donnie said.

"Can you do me a favor?" Jason asked.

"Huh?" Donnie replied.

"You're right above the shelf, can you get about fifteen meters above the surface?" Jason asked.

"Test where the turbines will rest?" Donnie said.

"Exactly," Jason replied.

"Raising the drone up," Donnie replied. "We're passed the space needed for the station, checking distance for turbines now."

The bottom of the rock bed slowly disappeared from view of the bottom camera, becoming an indiscernible shadow. Every view from the drone's cameras had a spotlight, then darkness. The front camera started to reveal the ridge, the inclining slope that marked the edge of where they could build.

"We're fifteen meters above the shelf, 20.12 meters per second," Donnie said. "Please leave enough room."

They watched the latitude and longitude as it shifted, the hundredth decimal shifting as the drone continued its journey.

"Twenty-one meters. We have twenty-one meters for a twenty-meter-wide turbine field down there," Donnie said. "Whoever has to place those turbines is going to hate us."

"But that's not our problem to deal with," Jason said.

"I think we should call Ronald McArnold back," Donnie said.

"Tell him our countdown to launch has begun?" Jason implied.

"Barring any weird discoveries, I think our countdown to building the largest and most powerful renewable energy station the world has ever seen has begun," Donnie smiled.

DAYS TO LAUNCH: 1277

The large warehouse Donnie and Jason entered housed several prototypes for the turbines. With saltwater, pressure from the ocean currents more intense and persistent than wind, and a number of other factors such as sediment, rock, and wildlife to account for, the number of problems they faced compared to solutions remained consistently lopsided.

The warehouse held nearly a dozen turbines, each one a quarter scale to fit within the space for testing purposes. In the rafters above was a cable rig to lift and move the various prototypes. On the east wall was a massive water tank. The high-tech setup had a huge generator behind it to simulate ocean currents. At the top was a hatch to lower and extract any of the prototypes in and out. Another water tank had several blades from different prototypes resting in churning water to test salinity and verify they could endure underwater. The blades stayed submerged to ensure the bearings to connect the blades to the nacelle wouldn't rust or deteriorate in the Pacific.

The turbines themselves sat two to a table. Each had different designs and technologies for the team to test and determine the ideal turbine to place at the bottom of the ocean. Some had the traditional three long blades, others had smaller ones, but more of them.

Donnie and Jason walked down a large set of stairs to see their two top engineers arguing again. On one side of a turbine, was Cody Seacrest, a larger kid with disheveled hair and a persistent unshaven look about him who'd recently graduated college. His loud antics and demeanor proved abrasive to most, but his knowledge of turbine technology was unparalleled. Opposite him stood Cameron Webb, an African American mountain who'd spent his young days aboard submarines; now, in his late forties, he still looked like he toiled over massive bolts and pipes all night and day. His working knowledge of the deep sea brought years of experience, which the kid didn't respond well to. Cameron calmly countered Cody's booming voice.

"The straight extension won't hold, the ocean is going to push and push those blades until they fracture or snap," Cameron said.

"That's what I'm trying to say, we can add feathering options so we can adjust the pitch angles to reduce pressure," Cody argued.

"Except we're not dealing with wind, we won't see mass variations – maybe some when there's a storm, but it'll be minimal because the turbines are so deep. We're talking about strong, persistent pressure that won't let up," Cameron said.

"So, we start with a feathered angle, then rotate the blade bearings, decrease our pitch angle until we see enough of a drop in pressure," Cody said, although his every word had the tone of yelling. Whispering wasn't in his skillsets. "Feathering doesn't have to be automated or adjustable; we can set them where we want and modify from there to deal with the inevitable variations we're going to see."

"Except you explained feathering decreases resistance so it'll spin slower, and I thought you wanted these to 'run free,'" Cameron said. "Plus, why add costs by adding variable bearings for speeds that are going to remain consistent? We're not exactly worried about cut-out speeds where we'll max these turbines out."

"Gentlemen, how's it coming?" Jason asked.

Both of them sighed, a groan even escaping Cody.

"Well, we've got most of the problems solved at this point," Cody said, then he pointed to a turbine in the southeast corner. "Number seven is the way to go for coating, we've tested salinity twenty percent above the water in the area the turbines will be placed, and it held up great. We've also got our concrete anchor and tethering system. They held even at sixty meters per second, three times what we're going to see, no signs of wear and tear."

"Excellent," Donnie replied.

"Yup, where we're running into trouble is the blades. Wind and water, especially at eight hundred and seventy-five meters down, function entirely different from one another." Cody pointed at the traditional, three-bladed turbine on a distant table. It'd been shuffled away once they knew it wasn't in contention. "The designs we have for wind aren't meant to endure the kind of pressure water brings, and although we figured out how to protect the turbines from the sides, a front and back grated shield to keep fish swimming in there or debris and sediment buildup is proving difficult. The prototypes we have right now are either too thin that stuff's getting through, or..."

"...or it's too protective and reducing the flow," Cameron added. "Other problem you just walked into was our blade system. Cody thinks we can have bearings to adjust the pitch angle and feathering but that isn't the issue for me – any blades sticking straight up, the edges are going to get thrust back by the current, no matter how much you adjust pitch and feathering or increase the base width."

"Tell you what," Cody said. "Let's put turbine six in the tank, that's got the widest base and also blade bearings so we can adjust. Let's test the theory."

"Wait, what am I hearing you propose?" Jason asked.

"Let's put debris in there, test it while we have the speed going at twenty meters per second, see what happens," Cody said.

"What happens if it breaks? It could cause major problems in the tank," Jason argued.

"Would you rather damage a test tank or have a blade snap and send shrapnel through a field of other turbines, domino into one another and destroy half the turbines or hit the station?" Cameron suggested.

"I'd rather be proven right, which I will be when we test it out," Cody replied. "It'll work out, the test tank is from the Navy. A few rocks won't damage it."

"What about uncontrolled, broken pieces of turbine blades?" Cameron asked.

"What about your face? It's going to be fine," Cody shot back. "I mean, your muscles would probably break the thing."

"You wanna test that theory?" Cameron asked.

"Yeah, I do." Cody walked over to the tank and gave it a couple slaps. "Throw you in there, see what it can take."

"What's that going to prove?" Cameron asked.

"It'll validate the sliding scale of what brings me total bliss while you get tossed around," Cody said.

"Okay, okay. That's enough," Jason intervened. "It's a test tank, so why don't we test it?"

"Cameron's face?" Cody asked.

"No!" Jason replied. "Get our operators in here to lift a turbine into the test tank, test your debris theory."

"We need some women on this team – there's too much testosterone going around," Donnie pleaded.

"Found a sister duo who are submersible drivers," Jason said. "Would be perfect for the dive crew."

"Oh, yeah, their resumes and experience seemed great. Plus, I'd welcome some calm heads for our first outside members diving to the station when it begins construction," Donnie said.

"Wait, we're not part of the dive crew that'll be on the station?" Cody asked.

"Not with this behavior – we need cool, collected heads down there," Donnie responded. "Not an arrogant college grad who won't admit he may be wrong and a smart, but stubborn as hell, overly jacked dude who should be a mentor."

The warehouse became awkwardly silent. The only sound was the water filters, churning the water in the two test tanks.

"Get the test going and figure this out, we're three weeks from turbine production starting so decisions need to be made," Jason said.

Jason and Donnie left the warehouse. They hopped into a golf cart to make their way over to the office building. They spoke as they drove outside the testing facility toward the corporate office building.

"You think they'll figure it out?" Donnie asked.

"Once they can solve their personal issues, absolutely," Jason said. "But you're looking at two fundamentally different lives trying to mesh. On one side, a kid who's been told he's a genius all his life and hasn't wanted for a thing because of it. Other side, you have a single father of three who learned as he went and fought for everything in his life, including this job."

"But they're both brilliant," Donnie said, turning the golf cart left and heading toward the security gate.

"Not denying that. You have a top turbine expert and someone whose engineering expertise fixed a stranded submarine in the middle of the Atlantic," Jason said. He showed his badge to the security guard.

Donnie did the same. "But it won't matter if..."

"It won't matter if they can't get along. The team we choose has to be able to handle the pressure of being almost nine hundred meters underwater with a thousand opportunities to screw something up that could kill you and the entire team in seconds," Jason said.

"Thank you for making me feel more at ease about going down there." Donnie waved at the security guard as he raised the barrier to the office building. "Thanks, Stan!"

"Well, we're going down there together," Jason said.

"Initially, then you're ditching me to come up to the Shore Station and run things from your cozy command center." Donnie parked the golf cart with the others. There were four of them for team members to take back and forth.

"Until the first rotation is up, then we swap," Jason said.

"Yeah, but talking about cool heads, yours is a lot cooler than mine," Donnie said. They entered the main door and headed for the elevators. "I mean that in multiple ways. I'm balding and looking more like my Uncle Melvin, you've got that gorgeous, flowing silver mane. You have a cooler head emotionally and literally."

"I do." Jason pressed the elevator button to their floor. "But that's why I'm overseeing things from the surface. I can keep it together and guide all of you."

"You think we'll find enough people to head down there? I mean, what sane person says 'Yup, think I'll go live in a submerged energy station at the bottom of the Pacific for a while, that won't be terrifying or dangerous at all,'" Donnie said.

The elevator reached their floor. The two stepped off and made their way toward their offices. As they walked, they saw Karina Lamott, one of the legal executives sitting on one of the benches. She swapped her heels for tennis shoes, pulling the comfortable option from her bag. She sniffled as she did, wiping a tear away while trying to hide it by brushing her hair back. She leaned over her knee to tie her tennis shoes.

Donnie stopped. He tapped Jason on his shoulder to wait a moment. "Karina, you doing okay?"

"Fine." Karina finished tying her second shoe. "Just having a Friday. How about you?"

"Yeah, having a Friday, too. Only thing our engineers seem to be interested in is engineering a way to tear each other's heads off," Donnie said.

"Ha, you think they'll figure it out?" Karina wiped her cheek again.

"Hope so, we had them allocated to be on the first rotation of the station team. Hoping they can work it out," Donnie said. "Can I get you a coffee or anything?"

"No, I'm okay." Karina stood, putting her heels in her large bag. "Hope they figure it out. Let me know if I can help. I may be joining you guys soon."

"How so?" Donnie asked.

"Oh, part of why I'm having a Friday." Karina waved her statement off. "You'll read about it, there's a company-wide email going out later today. Anyway, good luck. I'm around if you need anything."

"Okay, hope your Friday goes better," Donnie said.

He and Jason entered their office. A shared space, their desks faced one another, massive monitors on the right side of their desks. The two entered their respective passwords.

"Any idea what that was about?" Jason asked.

"No, although heard legal's been having some issues with clearing our cable runs to the shore, don't know the details, or if that's what it is at all. Wouldn't want their jobs in a million years. Glad they're doing it," Donnie said. "Hope she's all right."

"Yeah, me too," Jason said. "Do we have any replacements in mind if Cody and Cameron don't work out?"

"Not off the top of my head," Donnie said. "We need one for general engineering, another for energy and turbines, specifically. June would do well for general. Turbines, at that level of expertise, we're really only looking at Kyle. He's nice but…"

"Doesn't know how to handle a social situation if he had a gun to his head," Jason added. "Oh, you see the email from Cody? Looks like loading the turbine into the tank will take up the rest of the day. Testing in the morning. You okay with that?"

"I mean, I want a solution sooner rather than later, but I don't want to work the team after hours again, we're doing that too much already and we're not that far into this," Donnie replied.

Jason typed a reply. "Yeah, timing is tight, but we're not under the gun just yet."

"Tell Ronald that," Donnie laughed.

"After the last time trying to find a site, I'd like to avoid it. Hope tomorrow goes okay because I'm not enjoying the constant feeling of our jobs waiting for the big screw up to send us packing." Donnie stopped, wondering if that was what had bothered Karina so much. Did she lose her job or feel like she was almost done? The atmosphere of Maritimus Energy wasn't casual or relaxed, hadn't felt that way for some time. Donnie refreshed, waiting to see if the company-wide message she'd mentioned had been sent yet. Nothing.

The next morning, Donnie and Jason entered the warehouse. Again, Cameron and Cody were at it, but their tone seemed different. Cameron stood proud, looking the same day in and day out, cleanshaven and well-groomed. The tension on his shirt showed he'd already been to the gym early in the morning. It seemed no shirt fit him well. Cody was slumped over his computer, hair disheveled, five o'clock shadow from yesterday lingering. He wore aviator sunglasses as he entered commands into the test tank. But rather than standing opposite one another, they were side by side. They worked in tandem by the tank, Cody at the computer and Cameron activating the cameras that monitored the turbine inside the tank itself. The turbine was a one-quarter scale, otherwise they'd have to use an aquarium sized for a Beluga whale just to get the full turbine submerged. This allowed them to simulate oceanic circumstances, temperatures, salinity, and velocity of the current against the turbines without expensive installations or risking harming sea life and other aspects of the ocean just offshore.

The two engineers worked hard, not yet noticing that Donnie and Jason had entered the warehouse.

"Just take the sunglasses off. I don't know if you're trying to look like a rich asshole or a damned fool, but either way it's not an image any serious man wants," Cameron said.

"Here I thought I was going for a young, hefty Tony Stark." Cody pulled the sunglasses off his face.

"First you'd have to clean yourself up," Cameron replied. "Let's get the water churning, see what it does."

"Roger that," Cody said.

"Maybe splash some of it on your face, see if that wakes you up," Cameron joked.

"Roger that," Cody replied. "I think a full head dunk with the current flow simulation going. Get it going full speed!"

"Better than a cup of coffee, if you ask me," Cameron said.

The testing tank motors fired up. Watcher swirled about as the mechanized whir of the machines intensified. Cameron put earplugs in. He grabbed another pair, nudged Cody in the shoulder, and passed them over. As the exchange happened, Donnie and Jason walked down the stairs to greet them.

"Thanks, buddy!" Cody shouted. His voice could even be heard over the testing tank when working at full capacity. Cody put the earplugs in, pulling at his earlobes and making sure they were in securely.

"How's it coming?" Jason asked, having to shout.

"Good, just getting started," Cody replied.

Cameron gave them earplugs.

"Thank you," Donnie replied.

Jason nodded, a silent sign of his gratitude. Cody waved Donnie and Jason over to the computer, encouraging them to watch the data along with him. The water inside the testing tank moved at the equivalent of forty meters per second, testing the smaller-sized replica further than anything they'd experience on site where the station was going. However, the additional force allowed them to have contingency protocols in place and prove the turbines were capable of withstanding the force beyond a doubt.

"How long before we know how the turbine responds to the pressure?" Jason asked.

"There's a specific amount of resistance we know the turbine can take, we'll let it go full speed for a bit, then gauge to see how much torque is going on with the blades," Cody said. He took a large sip of coffee, then a swig of water, followed by a bite from a bagel with cream cheese. "We're at full speed."

Cameron grabbed his plate. He had an open-faced bagel with what looked like a dozen eggs, almost all whites, piled on top of it. Two over-easy eggs sat on top, the yolk dripping down the stack. He took a massive bite.

"Thanks for breakfast again," Cody said.

"What?" Cameron asked.

"I said thanks for breakfast!" Cody shouted.

"No problem," Cameron said. He looked at the readouts on his screen. "Seals and monitors are all doing great."

"We put seals in the tank?" Cody asked.

"Yeah, thought we'd see how marine life do getting hit by one of those things," Cameron said. "His name is Cody; he's a nice seal, but needs to get smacked around a little."

Donnie and Jason smiled, seeing a joking exchange between the two.

"Hey, Cody the seal may like to party and have fun with other seals, but he still comes in and gets the job done when he has to."

"Yeah, but a little slap upside the head every now and then could keep him in line," Cameron took another bite.

The turbine spun over and over, moving at a rapid pace and causing small white caps at the top of the waterline in the tank. As the pressure increased, Cody assessed.

"Well, it says it's holding, but this is with minimal timing and not the hundreds of variables we may face in the Pacific itself," Cody said.

"I want to tell you the blades are holding, and I would be right," Cameron said. "But at the same time, there's a ton we're going to see in reality we can't simulate in this tank."

Cameron looked around, trying to find something.

"What are you looking for?" Donnie asked.

Cameron went over to the side table where they initially set up breakfast. Cameron grabbed a small to-go mug of coffee.

"Cody, you done with this?" Cameron asked.

"I can be." He grabbed the mug, downed the rest, and handed it over to Cameron. "We doing this?"

"Think we have to," Cameron said.

"Wait, you're not putting a metal to-go mug in there?" Jason said.

"Would you rather put thousands of turbines that are four times larger and more expensive in the Pacific and watch them break one by one from disturbances we could test with a single prototype right now?" Cameron asked. "The kid's right."

"Yeah, we're going to have to make more once we decide on our final model, anyway." Jason squinted, looking at the near million-dollar testing tank and the six-figure prototype.

Cameron grabbed a ladder, placing it on the north side of the tank. He stood above the tank, a good twelve feet high. He raised a small panel, the opening to the testing tank. Cameron did not move the mug toward the opening, waiting for final clearance.

"Tell me when you're ready," Cameron said.

"Okay, reducing speed to twenty point five meters per second," Cody said. "Give it a minute. We'll start with anticipated speeds, see what that does, and go from there."

They paused for about a minute, waiting for the tank to reduce the speed. The white caps at the top turned to small splashes.

"No, wait!" Cody scanned the desk. "We should start with something smaller. Since the turbine's a quarter scale, that mug is almost a boulder. Let me find something that could be closer to sediment and rocks likely to flow through the current there."

It took a few minutes. Cody couldn't find anything that worked inside, so he ran to the door to grab some of the decorative stones used to frame the entrance alongside shrubs and trees. He held several in his hand.

"Doubt we'll hit it on the first try, so grabbed a bunch." Cody set them near the breakfast spread. A rock fell from his pile and smacked an open container of cream cheese, sending it off the edge of the table. "Damn it."

Cody reached down and picked the cream cheese up. Seeing a smear of white on the concrete floor, he looked over at his colleague. "Hey Cameron, you should come down. I think we should weigh these and identify them – that way we can see the impact and know for sure about weight ratios."

"Good thinking," Cameron said. "I was just excited to throw something in there."

"Oh, me too," Cody said. "But we should do it the scientific way, so we have strong data, not 'the rock broke the prototype.'"

The four of them worked quickly to make their charts. Jason created a labeling system, Cody weighed them all, Cameron marked them with a permanent marker, and Donnie logged their information into a shared document.

"Okay, they all ready and marked?" Cody asked.

"Yup, we're good to go," Donnie replied.

Cameron had a tray of decorative rocks; the light rose colored stones marked up with black ink to indicate their number. He carried the tray up the ladder, using one arm to hold the ladder, the other clinging to the tray as he climbed back to the top. He placed the tray on the top, away from the panel. He kept his grip loose for a moment, ensuring the tray was stable on the surface before working. After watching for a while, he knew the tray wasn't going anywhere so he lifted the panel.

"We ready?" Cameron asked.

"Ready! Shout the numbers out to me before you throw," Cody shouted from the floor.

"1A," Cameron said.

"1A," Cody said. "Confirmed. Launch it."

Cameron lowered his hand into the water, releasing the rock toward the south side where the turbine rested. The rock hit the tank's end.

"No impact," Cody said. "Throw 1B."

"Why a number and letter data set for labeling?" Donnie asked. "We're throwing rocks."

"In case we need to do another set should this not show us anything conclusive. Then we'll have '2A, 2B,' and so on until our theory is proven. But this way we'll also track our progress."

"1B, going in!" Cameron shouted. He lowered the rock into the water, nearly up to the elbow.

A higher pitched clank echoed in the tank, followed by a deep thud against the back side.

"Grazed blade two," Cody said. "Pressure and momentum remains unimpacted. We'll need some direct hits to be sure."

"1C, going in," Cameron said.

It missed entirely. 1D, 1E, and 1F all missed as well. 1G got them excited as it was another graze.

The eighth rock, 1H, was the larger one. Cameron lowered his arm into the water, feeling the increasing pull with repeated dunks into the tank. "Here it comes."

He let the rock go. Pulling his arm out, he shook it to get the water off and bring some warmth back into his fingers. Inside the tank was a huge clang.

"We've got a hit!" Cody shouted.

Cameron heard a rhythmic pounding against the tank. The hits came two at a time, before a lull. The two-one beat repeated, indicating the rock was stuck in a vicious cycle of hitting the blades and being tossed around.

"Hey, buddy, hop on down," Cody said.

Cameron stepped down the ladder quickly. Walking around, the source of the two hits, followed by the lull, came into view. He was wrong, it wasn't the rock stuck in a cycle. The sound was caused by one of the blades, which had been cracked. It slammed into the bottom rivet of the tank, shooting it upward. Then as it went up, it hit the wall of the tank, coming back to center for a moment until it slammed into the bottom rivet again.

"Damn," Cameron said.

"That rock weighed very little too," Cody said. "So…"

"So…" Donnie said.

"So…" Cody waved his arms in circles, encouraging them to say what he wanted to hear.

"Cody was right," Cameron said.

"Yeah!" Cody pumped his fist.

The turbine blade split further; now it dragged against the tank wall as it spun.

"Hey, Mr. Right?" Cameron said. "How about we shut the tank down before you're too right and we break the testing tank?"

"Oh, shit." Cody spun to his right, grabbing the controls to stop the water from moving. The turbine slowed, grinding against the wall to a slow and excruciating halt.

The four stood, looking at the scratches and dents against the tank and the busted prototype. Silence took over. The machine on the tank stopped. All that was left was the light wash of the water as the momentum slowed.

"Well, you proved the current prototypes can't take the impact," Jason said. "But here's the harder challenge…"

"What's that?" Cody asked.

"How do we fix it?" Jason asked.

"Right," Cody paused. "Right."

"Can you give us some time? Let us brainstorm and get back to you?" Cameron asked. "Maybe bring some ideas this afternoon?"

"Sure," Donnie replied.

"Think if we put our minds together, Cody and I can have at least some ideas the design team can explore," Cameron said.

"We've got a meeting at one, maybe after that?" Jason suggested.

"We'll have some ideas ready," Cody said. "They'll probably all be mine, but you know…"

"Please, you know the amount of submarines I've brought back from the dead? The tech may be different, but I've got decades of problem solving under my belt. You're just a baby when it comes to the actual work," Cameron said.

"Let's do this, then!" Cody shouted.

Donnie and Jason left the duo to keep working on a solution. They walked up the stairs to exit the testing facility while the engineers collaborated, giving one another grief as they did.

"What happened? Yesterday those two were ready to punch each other in the face," Donnie said.

"Think they realized they both want the same thing. They just get there in very different ways," Jason said. He looked down at the duo, who grabbed some pads of paper and pencils. They both sketched their ideas down. "Think they're focusing on what they both want, and finding a way to get there together, rather than insisting on their way being the only perspective on the table."

DAYS TO LAUNCH: 1162

The new prototype spun in the testing tank. Cody and Cameron's proposed solution came by angling the blades back – rather than rotating it on a bearing on a single pivot point, they created a ball bearing to tilt the turbine backwards, allowing the water to flow past it and not push directly against the current. The hope was that any debris would also glide off it, rather than slam into it. They also had three sets of blades put on the turbine to create a nine-blade system, feeding three generators. It meant a larger shell to protect the blades, but the manufacturing cost estimates were minor for added materials. To avoid the blades colliding with the backward-facing tilt, each set was built progressively smaller, providing space as they spun or rotated on the ball bearing.

The team of four tested the pressure – well, Donnie tried, at least. While Jason consulted with Cody and Cameron, he was stuck on the phone again with Ronald Arndt.

"Hey, Ronald," Donnie said. "Ronald?"

Donnie kept trying to get him to stop talking. He was frantic, worried about the manufacturing facility. It was scheduled to begin producing the full-sized turbines and needed approval on which prototype the team would use for the station in a few hours to guarantee on-time delivery.

Cameron stood atop a ladder again, panel open at the top of the test tank, several rocks in hand that had been labeled in permanent ink. He lined them up on the top of the tank, taking a sip of coffee from his to-go mug. He was feeling exhausted enough from the push to get the latest test done that he made the extra trip down the ladder to grab it.

"I understand, Ronald," Donnie said. "We're running impact tests, and once we're done with those, we'll know. Yes, they're highly sophisticated impact tests."

Donnie smiled, as did the rest of the team.

"Super sophisticated," Cameron said, lifting up his stack of stones with sharpie marks all over them.

"So sophisticated," Cody replied. His loud voice was enough for Ronald to hear over the phone.

"Yes, Cody was merely affirming the test's viability and method," Donnie said. He paused, listening to Ronald's rant continue. "Yes, Ronald. We know the deadline is coming up shortly. We'll get an answer to you as soon as we can."

Cameron leaned against the ladder, shaking his legs one at a time as the muscles tensed from standing on the tall ladder for so long.

"I don't know an exact time, Ronald," Donnie said. "The faster we can get the impact tests started, the faster we can get back to you. Yes, it is. Thank you."

Donnie hung up and sighed. "Next time, it's your turn."

"Next time learn how to win a game of rock, paper, scissors," Jason replied.

Donnie turned his cell phone off – if he couldn't see another call or email from Ronald, he didn't have to take it. "Ronald McArnold's a pain in the ass, but he isn't wrong. We've got to move. Where's the grate you talked about for the front and back of the shell?"

"Over there on the table, we'll test that next," Cody said.

"And you plan on the space between the grating being wide enough, so it won't interfere with current flow?" Jason walked over to a massive worktable, looking at the quarter-scale grate.

"Yep. It will allow for easy flow but stop anything of formidable size from entering. We'll have those in front and back to keep the current moving easily. Then the solid shell wrapping around the sides to attach the grating," Cody said.

"You know what I'd love?" Cameron asked. Jason, Donnie, and Cody turned to look. "For you guys to keep having this conversation while I'm standing on a twelve-foot-high ladder."

"Sorry, let's do the test," Cody said. "We want to test the strength of the new angled blades, without the grating."

"Okay, let's go," Donnie said.

As Cameron grabbed the first rock, Jason's phone vibrated. He pulled his phone out, reading through the notification. "Yeah, the head of the manufacturing facility is trying to reach me. They don't seem to listen to me when I tell them the more they ask, the longer this takes! Okay, let's move so we don't miss this deadline."

"5A," Cameron announced. "Dropping."

The rock, propelled by the momentum of the test tank, went away from the open panel, headed down the length of the long test tank, then hit against the back wall.

"Miss," Cody said. "All nine blades? Really? Huh."

"5B," Cameron said. "Dropping."

The rock hit against the first set of blades, and slingshot toward the top, launched by the impact. It hit the top of the tank, then drifted back down. The second set of blades chopped the rock to the side. The rock shot back, straight into the third set, then finally to the back of the testing tank.

"Whoa!" Cody shouted. "That was amazing!"

"How'd they do?" Jason asked.

"We saw an increase in pressure, but nothing even close to fracture," Cody said. "Let's make sure. Cameron, keep them coming!"

Cameron dropped rock after rock, a little more than half hitting at least one set of blades. The pattern they saw the most was if one set was hit, the rock would bounce around a bit, hitting more blades. However, the projectiles kept eventually reaching the back and the blades held strong.

Once all ten test rocks were "launched," Cameron made his way back down the ladder. He walked over to a happy trio.

"We have our turbine?" Cameron asked.

"We've got our turbine!" Cody raised his hands and the two met for a high five. "We'll test the grate to be sure it can withstand impacts as well, but it's a grate of welded metal. What's going to happen besides 'yes, it hit the grate?'"

"And hey! We made our deadline with thirty three whole minutes to spare before the manufacturing plant's deadline!" Cody said.

"So, what's next?" Donnie asked.

"We head down to the site, mark the official spots for construction," Jason replied.

"Did we hire our submersible drivers?" Cody asked.

"Yup, went with the Perez sisters," Donnie continued. "Their cognitive tests were through the roof, and they seemed to gel with all of us."

"That's great," Cameron said. "Was hoping it'd be them."

"We're going to the bottom of the ocean?" Cody hopped like a kid finding out they're going to the zoo. His large frame bounced with every impact on the ground.

"We're going to the bottom of the ocean!" Jason said.

The four celebrated for a moment, but then went right to their computers, not bothering to go to their respective offices. With emails and inquiries from the manufacturing plant they'd chosen to produce the turbines coming frequently, Jason wanted to send approval on the final design immediately to put everyone's mind at ease.

"I'll notify the manufacturer," Jason said. "Can you let Ronald McArnold and the execs know?"

"On it!" Donnie replied. "Wait, no. I'm not calling Ronald McArnold unless I lose."

Cody and Cameron stood side by side, watching the event unfold. "Isn't his name Ronald Arndt?"

"It is." Donnie readied for the challenge. "But demeaning him with a nickname makes us feel like we have some power over the situation. We have no time, one and done, agreed?"

"Agreed," Jason said.

They pumped their fists against their open palms three times, then revealed. Sure enough, Jason produced rock, Donnie tried scissors.

"Shit!" Donnie pulled out his cell phone to call Ronald.

He got a few seconds to speak, but before he was able to update Ronald, he had to pause while another rant started. As he did, Cody handed Jason a spec sheet.

"Yup, grate design thirty-six, shell 2A, turbine design G-2-A4," Jason said. "You okay to make a locking system for that grate and shell combination? Don't think those are the same."

Jason waited for a moment, as Donnie continued to get an earful from Ronald. "Hey, Ronald. Ronald? I'm trying to tell you we've got goo..."

"We've got 'goo?'" Cody asked.

Donnie shook his head.

Jason slapped the desk near him in celebration. "That's what I like to hear. You are good to start as soon as you are ready. No, thank you. Talk to you soon, I'm sure. You too."

Jason hung up. Donnie shook his head.

"Ronald, can I tell you something?" Donnie tried to interject. "Yeah, I want to share some good news."

As Donnie tried to make his voice heard, Jason mimed eating and whispered, "Something to eat?"

Donnie gave a thumbs up, and as they left, he mouthed, "I hate you."

Despite the long-winded rant from Ronald, Donnie had a moment of joy. He looked inside the test tank, seeing the three sets of blades still spinning slightly from the residual flow. He couldn't help but admire the turbine in front of him as the world's largest power station in existence was closer than ever to becoming a reality. But now they had to place thousands of them, alongside constructing a station, at the bottom of the Pacific.

DAYS TO LAUNCH: 982

The team was split in half, sitting in different submersibles within the dark of the ocean bottom. Two submersibles, the *Anaximander* and *Archimedes*, made their way to the coordinates where the station would be built. They had large, circular clear fronts, giving anyone in the submersible a wide view of the ocean ahead. Behind the "reverse fishbowl" were the engines and equipment. Several floodlights rested above and below them. On the bottom was a solid base, including two long mounts for when the submersible had to lay flat on the ocean bottom or get lowered onto a ship. Under the front space were two extendible claws to grab objects, maneuver, and manipulate, for occasions like when Donnie and Jason lost the unmanned drone to a strong surge of current, which sent them northwest, further from their destination than they intended. Their calculated drop wasn't enough to account for the massive pressure pushing them away from the west coast.

Jason and Cameron were in the *Anaximander*, piloted by one of two sisters, Juana Perez. She was an average height, unlike her formidable younger sister. The older of the two, she sported a black t-shirt to match her smooth hair. Her right arm had nearly an entire sleeve of tattoos. The forearm featured birds flying through the sky as the backdrop. The upper arm had geometric patterning, making the roses on her arm look like stained glass rising toward her shoulder, where a lion had been inked. The left arm had only one tattoo on the arm, "Emprender un Viaje," nothing more.

In the *Archimedes* was Donnie and Cody, piloted by the younger sister, Maria Elena Perez. She was considerably taller, pushing six feet. Her hair had a natural curl to it. Her eyes were a deeper brown, lips narrow, but equally full. She kept a consistent focus with wide brown eyes as she piloted the submersible.

"This is so amazing." Cody marveled at the pitch black surrounding them everywhere. Small specks of debris floated in front of them as they made their way past the gorges toward the flat rock bed they'd found earlier. "You just do this all the time?"

"This is one of the deeper dives I've done lately," Maria Elena replied. "We've been doing tours of wrecked ships right off the coast for rich tourists, call them 'richos' for short. Also did some dives for a documentary crew who're doing a nature series for a streaming network."

"Oh, which one?" Cody asked.

"Don't remember," Maria Elena replied. "Have it in an email somewhere. It won't be out for a while. They've got more shoots in the rainforest, while another crew's headed to Antarctica."

"How's the ice shelf doing?" Cody asked.

"Nearly gone," Maria Elena replied. "They said the script for that episode is going to have the 'last glimpse of a dying world' vibe."

"That's insane," Cody replied. "It's completely bonkers that if I have kids, I could raise them in a world with only six continents."

"My kids are ten and twelve," Donnie chimed in. "I'm glad they were able to be around while it was still here."

The three sat in silence. Maria Elena was used to it, spending hours on end inside the submersible. Donnie and Cody couldn't stop looking around. Even shrouded in darkness, the silhouette of the gorge near them emerged as the submersible passed the rocks and ocean bottom. The curve of the rock's edge slanted up as the flat area came into view.

"This is it?" Cody asked.

"This is it," Donnie replied. He looked over at the submersible driver. "Where do you want to start?"

"We'll start here near the edge, map out the first turbine field, then work our way in," Maria Elena said.

"What if we reach the ridge and find out we don't have enough room?" Donnie asked.

"Same outcome as if we started at the ridge and worked our way over here – this cuts travel time and we don't have much with how long that unexpected trip took," Maria Elena said.

Donnie smiled, looking over at Cody. "And that's why you trust the experts."

"Juana, I'm going to stay here, can you caddy corner me?" Maria Elena radioed.

"Twenty over, sixty up, right?" Juana asked.

"You got it." Maria Elena used the motorized arms to reach into a storage container on the outside hull. Using an adjustable claw, she gripped a long, steel rod with electronic sensors and transmitters on it. "These stakes are great, Cody."

"Thanks, it's going to make gridding this so easy," Cody said. "Flannery helped develop this app. Wish she could come with us!"

"She hasn't gone through the dive training yet," Donnie said. "But she will."

"Anyway, I've got my computer up, so I can keep track," Cody said.

Maria Elena pushed the stake into the silt below. A cloud of dust rose up, covering the clear globe-like viewport in front of them.

"You have it?" Maria Elena asked.

"Tracking," Cody said. "Once Juana extracts and activates hers, we should start receiving grid coordinates. From there we'll be able to map exact spots for every turbine."

Ahead of them, Juana piloted the other submersible. The lights made her shine all through the space, the only source of brightness outside of their own spotlights. Cody monitored the distances as she went toward her destination. Juana brought out the other stake.

"Okay, I'm at eighteen point five meters wide and fifty-six meters length, adjusting," Juana radioed. "Almost there."

As Juana moved to adjust her distance, Maria Elena pulled another stake to make her way to a third corner and marked the spot. She used the motorized claw to reach under.

Cody pointed out toward the rock bed. "The ground. Is it just me or is it moving?"

"Eyes play tricks on you sometimes down here." Maria Elena looked up. "Sure it's just…"

Maria Elena stopped; Cody wasn't wrong. The silt and sand did move, but it wasn't erratic. There was a distinct pattern to the movement. "Look at those long, floppy limbs. We've got an octopus coming over to see what the hell's going on."

Maria Elena moved the submersible back. The octopus adapted its skin to match the rocks and silt, making it hard to discern, especially as the submersible kicked up more of the ocean bottom. The cloud caused the octopus to freeze. It remained in place, waiting in camouflage for the small cloud of debris to settle and to know it wasn't in danger.

"Maria Elena, what's going on?" Juana asked.

"I've got a visitor, an octopus. Camouflaged. Backing up to give it some space," she replied.

As the cloud settled, the octopus moved toward the stake. The transmitter had a few blinking lights on it. Maria Elena kept the submersible floating just near the edge where the flat met the gorge. The port side of the submersible hung over the open space below.

"Does it think it's prey?" Donnie asked.

"Could be confusing it for bioluminescence, this deep there could be some fish that use it for hunting or defense," Maria Elena said. "Jeez, that's a big one. Must like the deeper water."

The long tentacles wrapped around, then forward as it edged closer to the stake. It wrapped around the bottom base gently.

"Is it going to be a problem if it breaks the stake?" Maria Elena asked.

"Well, kinda late to ask that question," Cody laughed.

"True," she replied.

"We have two spares per submersible, we're fine," Cody replied.

"Let's get a closer look." Maria Elena readjusted her grip on the controls. She moved a spotlight to better see the octopus.

It wasn't the reddish-brown normal color. The shade matched the beige and grey of the ocean bottom to remain as hidden as it could. It tested the stake a bit more as the spotlight moved toward it. The suction cups grabbed the stake, extracting it from the surface.

The spotlight illuminated the octopus fully. It flinched, angling toward the submersible. It darted away, launching the stake out of its grip and firing ink from its body.

"Damn," Maria Elena said. "Whoa."

The stake floated toward the submersible, launched by the octopus. The fast current pushed the stake straight into the submersible, entering the portside thruster. The thruster immediately died, falling apart as the spinning pieces ripped one another apart.

"Hang on," Maria Elena said.

The entire submersible tilted down and to the left. The starboard thruster pushed with no resistance from the other side, launching the bow left and down. As they swung, the current caught the starboard wall of the submersible. It pushed them down into the gorge.

"I got this." Maria Elena worked on correcting their course. The thrust of the increasing current kept them going straight into the gorge.

"Brace, brace," Maria Elena said as calmly as she talked about placing the stake.

The stern of the submersible scraped against the rock behind them. It swung them around again, the bow facing the deepening gorge. Maria Elena pushed the controls hard, trying to keep the starboard thruster from propelling them in a circle toward the gorge wall again.

The port side hit the rocks, but the momentum kept them going forward. Pieces of rock and clouds of silt flew off the gorge walls.

"Slow down!" Donnie yelled.

"It's the current. I'm already in reverse," Maria Elena said. "We've got to get to a clearing."

The grinding sound of rock against metal echoed into the submersible interior at a deafening rate. The crunch and squeal dissipated as Maria

Elena corrected the submersible's course. Ahead, the gorge narrowed, walls of rock squeezing closer and closer.

"Going up." Maria Elena pulled the submersible higher. As it propelled forward to the narrowing gorge, she listed it as much as she could to avoid a nasty impact. The bottom container on the submersible clanged against the narrowing stretch. The bow swung down from the hit.

Maria Elena pushed against the downward momentum. After the narrow wall stretch, the gorge widened. The rocks spread out and down in a strong slope, leaving a massive gulch that led out to the ever-deepening Pacific. The submersible crawled slower and slower until it came to a stop.

Maria Elena exhaled for what felt like the first time in a minute. "Fucking octopus. Throwing shit at me."

She checked gauges, status of the other thrusters, verifying if the remaining equipment was intact. "See what I do next time I want to observe the beauty of goddamned nature."

"You okay?" Donnie asked.

"Yeah, just pissed off," Maria Elena said. "What about you two? You doing okay?"

"I thought you said, 'you got this?'" Donnie asked.

"I did. I kept the impacts to the back, sides, and bottom to avoid our glass viewport getting smashed open and letting the whole Pacific in here," Maria Elena explained.

"Oh, you did have it," Donnie said.

"What about you, Cody?" she asked.

"That," Cody paused, "was awesome!"

He let out a huge laugh, issuing little shots of breath as he smiled ear to ear. "Man, that was crazy. The submersible okay?"

"It will be," Maria Elena replied.

"Maria Elena, where'd you go?" Juana radioed.

"Hey, octopus got scared, was seeing what the stake was because of the light, then it bolted and launched the stake into my port thruster," Maria Elena replied.

"No," Juana said.

"Right? So, we lost control, got pushed into the gorge. I'm down in the opening now with only two stern thrusters," Maria Elena responded.

"What a little shit," Juana said.

"Who?" Maria Elena replied.

"The octopus," Juana said.

"Total shit," Maria Elena said.

"What's your status?" Juana asked. "Do you need a tow?"

"No, we can make it back up. You going to keep mapping out the construction zones?"

"We lost so much juice going against the current after the descent," Juana said. "Think we can get one grid marked, after that I need to make my way to the surface, recharge. We should get you fixed up, start again later this week."

"Agreed," Maria Elena said.

"Later this week?" Donnie asked.

"Yeah," Maria Elena shot a few dark looks from her large, brown eyes. "You know how to replace a submersible thruster?"

"Fair enough," Donnie nodded.

"That's the second time you've questioned me in my own sub." Maria Elena engaged the thrusters to raise the submersible. She kept the entire thing from spinning by disengaging the starboard thruster and making minor adjustments with just the center stern thruster to adjust their alignment. The rest was up to the bottom thrusters. "You need to trust me when I'm piloting this thing."

"Yup," Donnie said.

"She kept us from getting ground down into mincemeat while we were launched through the gorge," Cody said.

"And I've gotten out of hairier situations than that," Maria Elena said. "We good?"

"Yeah, we're going to be great," Donnie said. "Thank you."

The *Archimedes* rose toward the surface, signaling for the research vessel to start heading northwest to retrieve them. Below, the water continued to flow, waiting until they returned to test them again.

DAYS TO LAUNCH: 652

The stars were hindered by floodlights, cranes, and moving machinery. They drowned out visibility to the world above. Donnie and Jason walked together along the loading docks, while a night crew prepared the station shell to load onto a ship. Six massive pieces rested in a line on the dock. The bottom left, bottom right, top left, top right, conical-shaped front, and wide rectangular rear panel for the cargo bay rested in succession, each waiting their turn to get put onto the *Boundless*, a ship brought over from the Chinese government, and the only one capable of lowering cargo to a depth of one thousand meters. From there, they'd bring the station shell to the bottom of the Pacific in the morning. The site at the ocean bottom had been prepared, concrete bases in place.

Crews fixed harnesses and loading straps to the bottom left panel. Twenty-nine meters long, half as wide, the rectangular piece was the first to get taken to the bottom tomorrow. Another panel would be sent every day for six days straight. The night crew was responsible for placing the panel on the boat, then in the early morning the *Boundless* would leave the dock and make its way to the station site. Another ship, the *Merriweather*, would provide assistance and counterbalance for initial lowering, making sure the panel entered the water with ease using additional cranes and pulleys, ensuring the *Boundless* wouldn't tip from such weight.

"Can't believe this," Jason said.

"I know. It felt surreal when the turbines started going down there. But there's something about the station being lowered that makes it seem that much closer to becoming a reality. Hard to comprehend we're at this stage," Donnie replied.

The two stood a good twenty meters from the ship and the individual pieces, not allowed anywhere close to the massive equipment and moving pieces and crew. Even from that distance, they could hear the dock foreman ordering their crew about to various spots. A few dock workers climbed massive walkways and ladders toward the top of the operating cranes to move the bottom left panel aboard the *Boundless*.

"How close are they?" Cody's voice boomed from practically the back entrance to the dock.

Donnie and Jason turned, seeing Cody, Cameron, Juana, Maria Elena, and Ava Flannery all walking together. Cody carried several bags of food with him. Cameron had one drink caddy, Maria Elena the other.

"Not sure. Seeing some crew entering the cranes, so can't be too long now," Donnie said. "And whoa, our Silicon Valley superstar is gracing us with her presence!"

Flannery nodded and smiled. Her thin, wide smile remained closed – she hardly ever showed her teeth, not through talking, smiling, or laughing. Every movement of hers was subtle, no matter how animated or intense she got while working. It made her a prominent voice, but never a loud one among the crew. Her jet-black hair and dark brown eyes juxtaposed against her pale white skin. "Yeah, you know I can't avoid a spectacle of any kind."

She wore her usual light blue jeans, comfortable boots, and black shirt, sleeves short enough to show off her tattoos, something her and Juana bonded over.

"No Karina?" Donnie asked.

"Nope, we asked her though." Cody handed out bags of food to everyone. The group found a few planks on the dock where they could sit and watch the panel get loaded. "You think she'll ever feel like a part of the crew?"

"I'm sure she'll come around," Jason said, taking his meal from Cody as he handed it over. "But her position with corporate puts her in an odd situation, too."

"How is the ship not going to tip when it lowers that panel into the water?" Cody asked.

"Cranes on the opposing sides." Cameron pointed over to the port side. "They'll raise it from the port side, but lower it on the starboard, that way the weight of the ship will counterbalance. That and the *Merriweather* will do the same on the opposite end, offsetting the weight and creating a nice, even distribution. Once it's in the water, the crane system will keep just enough tension to lower the panel but not drop it."

"With all the panels lowered and assembled, we can use the pumps to clear the station, start bringing in tech through the cargo bay in the back," Jason explained.

"I'm glad I came along," Flannery said. "Although, Cody, where's my food?"

"Hang on." Cody struggled as he looked at the bottom of another bag. "I can't tell which one is the veggie burger."

"Green wrapper," Flannery replied.

"Thank you." Cody handed a bag to Flannery. "Rest are double cheeseburgers for everyone who didn't specify."

Cody held on to one bag while Donnie and Maria Elena grabbed the other two. Juana fished through the second bag for her meal. Cameron distributed drinks, giving out the different cups. Meanwhile, more sounds came from the dock, the hydraulic pistons activating, cranes rotating, dock workers talking amongst themselves, and a foreman overseeing everything.

"Thanks for picking up food, guys." Jason unwrapped his chicken sandwich.

"We already had the show, might as well add dinner to it," Cody said, a mouthful of cheeseburger already in his mouth.

"Everyone feel comfortable with the early morning call to be back here?" Donnie asked.

"It'll be fine, lack of sleep is worth it. At least for this first panel load-in. No one has done cargo offloading in the water with anything close to this size," Cameron said.

"Well, stop handing out drinks and watch before they move it and you aren't paying attention," Juana said.

"I'm trying, I'm trying." Cameron handed the last drink to Jason.

"Doesn't help that your giant, muscly ass body is blocking everyone's view," Maria Elena joked.

"Knowing you, this meal will go straight to your pecs," Cody laughed.

The crew sat in silence after that, enjoying the cool breeze, saltwater coming off the waves splashing against the dock, watching the night crew load the panel onto the *Boundless*.

"How's recruiting for the secondary crew going?" Cameron asked.

"Moving along," Jason said. "Kind of wish I could just head down there with all of you for this first six-month rotation."

"Eh, you'll get to know your new crew and be glad you sent Donnie down with us first," Cody said, another bite of his burger in his mouth muffling every syllable.

"True words," Jason said. "Otherwise I'm going down there with my partner who annoys me, a loudmouth, Silicon Valley hothead, the sisters who give out more sass than I ever needed and…"

He raced through his brain, trying to think of something to say about Cameron.

"Nah, you won't be able to come up with anything. Everyone wants to work with Cameron," Juana said.

The entire group agreed. Cameron blushed, smiling as he tried to wave off the sea of compliments being thrown at him.

"I know the work dynamic will change once you start heading down there regularly, but I'll still do periodic trips, plus I'll be checking in from Shore Station," Jason said.

"Asking too many damned questions," Cody added.

"So many questions!" Maria Elena added.

After the grief and noise died down, Cameron jumped in. "You do annoy the hell out of all of us with your questions. But, it's just because you want to make things the best they can be all the time."

"I don't mean to annoy you guys," Jason said.

"'You guys?'" Flannery shot a pointed glare at him, a smile underneath it.

"Everyone. I don't mean to annoy everyone," Jason said.

"Thank you, Jason," Flannery replied.

One of the cranes clicked into gear. The harnesses tightened. The group got quiet as another crane locked its harnesses. Two final cranes pulled into position, increasing the tension, ready to raise the panel onto the *Boundless*. Far in the distance, they could hear the foreman verifying all parties as ready. Then, they could make out the foreman's voice as they shouted the countdown, using a megaphone to make sure no one misunderstood their commands.

"Five, four, three, two, one, and lift!" the foreman shouted.

Machines kicked to life everywhere. The four cranes on either corner groaned against the agonizing strain of lifting tons of metal off the ground. The cranes moved up toward a massive series of metal rafters that hung over the ship. One side of the rafters was welded to the dock, anchoring it to land. Those beams went up to another set that rested over and above the *Boundless*, going straight out to guide the panel over the ship. Then at another junction, the beams went into the ocean, placed onto concrete anchors in the water below. The *Boundless* rested between the beams and the dock, scaffolding welded above them to bring the massive cargo loads straight down onto the ship's deck.

The cranes lifted the large piece of the station. The panel came up to the starboard side of the ship.

"Cranes, hold," the foreman ordered. "Loading team, latch on port side."

A few dockworkers walked along the rafter railings, guiding the cables to the loading beams. More harnesses came down and latched onto the panel from the welded loader.

"Hold," the foreman shouted. "Loading team, latch on starboard side."

Once one side was locked, the cables and harnesses shuttled the panel toward the center of the ship; as the other side reached the loader, the movement stopped to allow dockworkers to transfer the other harnesses onto the panel.

"What if the panel just came off the harnesses and fell straight into the water or crashed onto the *Boundless*?" Cody asked.

"Cody!" Jason shook his head. "Can we not present scenarios in which the project gets completely derailed?"

"So you're saying we have a spare panel somewhere?" Cody took a bite.

"Tons," Donnie said. "We could ruin this station fifty times over and not worry about a thing."

"Good to know," Cody said.

"It is too bad Karina chose not to come along," Donnie said. "Would've been nice, especially since she's part of the initial dive team."

"To be fair her situation was pretty rough, can't blame her for feeling like she's all alone," Jason replied. "The entire dynamic of her work was changed and she was pulled off the legal team at basically a moment's notice."

With all the harnesses on the loader completed, the hydraulics engaged to move the panel over the *Boundless* deck.

"Wait," Flannery stopped eating. "Our corporate liaison is from legal? They didn't assign someone from operations who could contribute or PR to be the face of the dive team?"

"Loading team, hold there!" the foreman ordered. "*Boundless,* confirm teams are in position and ready."

"I'm sure the board had its reasons," Donnie said. "Plus, who can sell ideas and spin better than a lawyer? I've worked with her in the main office, she's got a lot to say and it's all really smart and well-informed. So let's give her the space she's asking for and trust that she'll come around. Yes?"

The team all nodded. The hydraulics kicked in, and the harnesses lowered the panel to the *Boundless.* The ship waited and crew members stood by the various base mounts to secure the massive span of metal in place.

Donnie took a bite from his burger, smiling as he watched the panel make its way to the ship. There, with the rest of the crew he'd be diving with to the bottom once the station was done and the energy expert who initially came to him with this idea and opportunity from Maritimus Energy, he couldn't help but enjoy the moment.

"Man, don't see how I'll sleep tonight," Donnie said.

The panel landed on the base mounts. The entire ship tilted down from the weight, receiving an entire freight shipment in one move. Water splashed up onto the docks from the swell caused by the *Boundless'* sudden drop.

"*Boundless,* remove the harnesses," the foreman ordered.

The dive crew of six sat together, absorbing the scene as the ship's crew tethered the panel down using hooks on the underside of the panel. No one would be able to bring straps over it – it was too large for any human to crawl over.

"Juana, Maria Elena, how are you feeling about tomorrow?" Donnie asked.

"Fine," Maria Elena replied. "Between the two of us, we've done this almost eight thousand times with the turbines now. It's the same process, only with an object about twenty times larger than one of the turbines."

"No pressure," Cody said. "Hey, what if…"

"Cody!" Jason interrupted. "Just don't."

The six enjoyed their night, absorbing the spectacle before they began spending nearly every day for the foreseeable future at the bottom of the Pacific Ocean, in an attempt to get the station ready and generate more renewable energy than the world had ever seen.

DAYS TO LAUNCH: 651

Maria Elena had performed dives hundreds of times now, dozens to the station site alone. Yet she couldn't help checking the gauges, monitoring the descent, and keeping a continuous eye on every aspect of the dive possible. She'd reached the rocky flat, and hovered near her concrete base for the incoming panel from the surface. She kept replaying Cody's jokes about things going wrong, the panel falling off the *Boundless* or something ridiculous. With each replay, she had an equivalent scenario where something she did during this load-in would cause the panel to get destroyed or damaged, hindering the entire project. Cody never meant harm in his jokes, but he rarely thought about what he said before shouting it out.

She looked to her right, at Cameron sitting next to her. It was just the two of them in the *Archimedes*. Donnie and Jason remained topside to oversee lowering from the *Boundless* into the water. Karina spoke to the press about the big day. Flannery retreated to keep working on the operating systems – she had time to finish since their main computer wouldn't be lowered until well after the station shell was built and put together. Juana and Cody were in the *Anaximander*. The new recruits who'd be on the surface team when the station launched were in two other submersibles, the *Proclus* and the *Plutarch*. They were piloted by Ateera and Kit. Ateera had facts about the ocean and its marine biology at the ready any time. She could quirkily spout out trivia on whales as quickly as she could tell you her mother's name. Kit sported thin wire-framed circular glasses, and a beard that went well below his collar bone. His hair nearly to his shoulders, everyone mistook him for a raging liberal. He was full of common sense, and therefore argued constantly against the two-party system in America. The two were a wealth of knowledge for anyone with a listening ear. Between the four submersibles, every pilot had a corner to manually lower the panel into place.

"ETA to panel arrival, two and a half minutes," Donnie said.

"Two and a half minutes, roger that," Juana replied.

Maria Elena's older sister was responsible for the dive team. She was chosen to command and oversee all four submersibles for the panel lowering. It was the logical choice; she'd always put more on her shoulders than Maria Elena thought she should bear.

"*Proclus*, adjust your setting; move a quarter of a meter south and east, you want the panel to be close, not land on you," Juana said. "We can adjust once it's lowered."

"Copy that, *Anaximander*," Ateera replied.

Maria Elena wondered if the fact they gave the station and submersibles official names for this trip made things seem all that much more real and therefore played into why she felt so nervous this time around. It was the biggest dive of her life. Yet, she'd had at least a dozen of the "biggest dives" in the eight years she'd been piloting submersibles. She achieved one goal, moved on to the next.

"Ninety seconds, team," Donnie said. "Panel should be in sight in sixty."

Maria Elena looked up, knowing she wouldn't see a thing for some time. Anxious, she turned toward Cameron.

"How you doing, Cameron?" she asked.

"Well, I'm doing alright," he replied. "How about yourself?"

"Medium," Maria Elena replied. "Turbines were turbines, I've loaded items larger than those before. This one…"

"Feels different," Cameron replied.

"Yeah." Maria Elena kept her eyes up top. When she didn't see anything, she swapped to the monitors, looking at the feed from the top camera.

"I get it, I was on submarines in the Navy, saw combat conditions, you name it. This one has a different feel about it," Cameron said. "Not more dangerous, or any less important, but different."

"Unknown," Maria Elena replied.

"Exactly, it's never a familiar feeling when you're doing something no one else has," Cameron said. He pointed to one of the monitors, displaying the camera pointed straight up. "Oh, panel is in sight."

Through the floating silt and specks, a massive silver silhouette appeared against complete shadow, its descent slow and consistent.

"*Boundless*, this is *Anaximander*," Juana radioed. "Panel is in sight. Repeat, panel is in sight."

"Copy that, *Anaximander*," Donnie responded. "Descending to eight hundred and seventy meters before stop."

As it approached the concrete bases, one for each corner and a few in between, the panel's descent slowed even more. The ship above decelerated the winches to bring the last few meters to a crawl.

"All subs, back up just a bit," Juana ordered. "Don't want any sudden current swells pushing this panel right into you. Let's make sure it's settled first."

Maria Elena grabbed the controls, reversing her submersible. The spotlights of the other three went further from her, becoming fainter in the dark ocean. It never took much to disappear into shadow at the bottom of the ocean. She stopped her submersible, holding strong a few meters away, and through the top of the front glass they could see the panel as it approached.

The panel rivaled the size of a large blue whale – if one swam by, they'd be a close comparison. Maria Elena did not miss the days of performing dives for rich tourists, but she did love the sight of incredible animals in the ocean – when they didn't launch equipment into her submersible, that is. It had been a while and she looked forward to the days her dives included some lighter blue water, a reef, or watching a pod of whales move by the glass of a submersible.

She extended the mandible claws, getting ready to help guide the panel down. Maria Elena hovered the *Archimedes* above the ocean floor. In front of her was a challenge no submersible driver had ever faced. She sighed in anticipation, then a smile escaped her, knowing when the story of the largest renewable energy station ever conceived was written, her contribution would be a part of it. No one would be able to take that from her.

"Okay, almost there," Donnie radioed from the surface.

The panel crawled, inching along through the last meter until it finally stopped.

"*Anaximander*, we have stopped. Showing we're at 870.25 meters," Donnie said. "Do you need us to retract for exact eight hundred and seventy meters?"

"Negative, *Boundless*," Juana replied. "We've still got room to maneuver. *Proclus*, *Plutarch*, maneuver to your corners first."

In the distance, two of the submersibles, caddy-cornered to one another, moved in toward the panel. As they clamped down on the handles with their hydraulic grips, Maria Elena could hear subtle echoes through the deep.

"*Plutarch* is attached," Kit radioed.

"*Proclus* is attached," Ateera followed shortly after.

"*Archimedes*, it's our turn," Juana radioed.

Maria Elena brought her submersible up, then forward. She pushed the mechanized claws out. As she got closer, the mounting grips came into view.

"Need me to navigate the claws while you drive?" Cameron asked.

"Got it, thanks though," Maria Elena replied.

"No problem," Cameron said. "Just let me know what you need."

She nodded, concentrating on the task ahead. The *Archimedes* sped toward the panel faster than Maria Elena liked from the current's momentum pushing against it. She reduced the forward momentum on the back thrusters to a comfortable speed for her.

"*Anaximander* is attached," Juana replied.

Maria Elena reached the claws out. The mounting grips were small handles welded to the body of the panel. The two sides of the claw went over and under the handle. She squeezed the grip on the controls. The claws tightened on the two mounting grips; the echo from their anchoring was loud, yet still muffled by the water, like the sound of a hammer falling to the bottom of a full tub.

"*Archimedes* is attached," Maria Elena radioed.

"Well done, team," Juana replied. "We're off from our landing points to mount the bases. Hold fast, we're going to have to shimmy with the panel. I'm about two meters too far up and over. *Archimedes,* where are you at?"

Maria Elena looked down below. She couldn't even see her concrete base through the viewport, the giant globe-shaped front that gave a decent view of all major angles.

"Hold tight, *Anaximander.* Getting exacts for you." She turned to Cameron. "Hey Cameron, can you use the bottom camera to find the concrete base?"

"On it." He pulled up the monitor on his side, firing up the controls for the camera. After gaining control of the system, he navigated the camera, looking around.

"Any luck?" Maria Elena asked.

"Not seeing it," Cameron said.

"You on the bottom center camera?" she asked.

"Yup," he answered.

"Swap to bottom rear camera," she suggested. Knowing her older sister was seconds from checking in, she radioed to get ahead of it. "*Anaximander,* our back is to the concrete base, using the bottom cameras to get you an answer. Hold tight, please."

"Copy that," Juana replied. "*Proclus, Plutarch,* get me your distances and alignment as well. The two of us should be enough but I'd rather be sure. *Boundless* has a fat ass so I don't want to ask them to move topside three times or anything."

Cameron adjusted the camera controls while watching the monitor with intent – it was nearly in a blind spot between the center and rear bottom cameras. "Here you go."

"Okay." Maria Elena pulled up a grid on the computer, looking at the signal indicator on the panel mount, then gauging it against the concrete base's location. "*Anaximander*, this is the *Archimedes*. I'm just over two and a half meters off. So that half meter from my side to yours shows we not only have to fix distance, but we're also not lined up straight."

"*Boundless*, you reading us?" Juana radioed.

"Copy that, we're pulling up all four of your alignments now," Donnie said. "Then we'll adjust."

Minutes passed. The two sat in silence inside the *Archimedes*. Cameron coughed, clearing his throat, then decided to break the quiet atmosphere. "If an octopus could get breakfast, what do you think they'd order?"

Maria Elena smiled. "You said 'order,' so you're suggesting he's in a diner or something, right? Not cooking at home?"

"Yes," Cameron said. "An octopus is capable of entering a diner, getting a table, and reading the menu. What does he order?"

"Well, I'd say a steak because one tried to eat one of our stakes that one time." They smiled. She thought about her answer for a moment. "The number eight."

"Because he's an octopus?" Cameron asked.

"You got it," Maria Elena replied.

"What's on a number eight?" he asked.

"No idea, but whatever it is on the menu, he's having it!" She felt tension on the mechanized arms. She loosened the claws on the mounting grip, letting the flow of the ocean current move a little easier.

"Next time I'm at a diner, I'll do the same. Won't matter what's on it, I'll just order it," Cameron responded.

"We have our alignments ready, adjusting the cranes now," Donnie radioed. "Go ahead and release the mounting grips, we'll reset once the panel settles."

"Roger that," Juana replied. "All submersibles, back up seven and a half meters, let's triple the wiggle room for how far they have to go in case the current kicks up or anything."

The submersibles retracted, waiting for the *Boundless* to adjust the panel. The time it took for the cranes to engage then see movement on the harnesses was minutes. With eight hundred and seventy meters' worth of cable, each shift moved subtly and took time.

Maria Elena looked at the alignment. It was improving, but as she scanned the bottom cameras, the panel didn't seem quite right.

"You okay?" Cameron asked.

"I don't know. They're still adjusting but we're not getting close enough, something feels off," she replied. "It'll be fine. It'll work out."

A few more minutes passed. The Shore Station helped relay additional calculations for adjustment to the *Boundless*. After some time, the radio fired back up.

"*Anaximander*, this is the *Boundless*," Donnie said. "We have made adjustments; can you confirm alignment?"

"All submersibles, check in," Juana radioed. "*Anaximander* is looking aligned."

"*Proclus* is aligned," Ateera replied.

There was a silence from the *Plutarch*. Maria Elena analyzed her approach, checking the monitors regarding the mounting bracket with the concrete base. The long rod-like piece coming out of the concrete to go into the bracket looked close, but not quite right.

"*Archimedes, Plutarch*. How are we looking?" Juana asked.

"This is the *Archimedes*. I'm looking mostly aligned. May be the angle, can't quite tell," Maria Elena said.

"Do you need adjustments?" Juana asked.

"We're still three meters above the concrete base's top edge, think I'll know if we get closer," she responded.

"*Plutarch*?" Juana asked for the second opinion.

"Yeah, feeling the same way. Doesn't seem perfect, but we've got some room with the bracket," Kit said.

"What are we doing then?" Donnie asked.

"Maria Elena? You've got eyes on your base," Juana radioed.

Maria Elena brought her finger to the monitor where it showed the mounting bracket on the panel, and she moved her finger down toward the concrete base. It was so close, yet it wasn't quite aligned.

"Let's bring it down a meter and a half," Maria Elena suggested. "Halve the distance to get a better look."

"Copy that," Juana responded. "*Boundless*, bring the panel down one point five meters."

The minutes passed until the action showed on their end. Then the panel stirred, coming down in the deep. The circular mounting bracket crept toward the concrete base rod. As it approached, Maria Elena saw how close they were, but it wasn't right. The panel stopped, with one point five meters to go.

"Yeah, *Anaximander*, this is the *Archimedes*. We're still several centimeters off. The edge of the rod will either hit, or grind, the bracket on the south side," Maria Elena radioed. "Looking like five to six centimeters off from the rod's edge."

"*Plutarch*?" Juana radioed.

"Not as much, I'm looking at four to five centimeters, south as well," Kit said.

"I'm dead center," the *Proclus* radioed.

"I'm about three centimeters off center, but that's more than enough to mount and seal," Juana radioed. "Am I the only one confused by the math?"

"Do you think the bases settled more? Some of the top-layer sediment is pretty loose," Maria Elena said.

"Except we cleared it before lowering, and we did realignments yesterday," Juana said.

Maria Elena pulled up the four concrete bases. They were all in exact position. "Bases are in the right spot, center bases look perfectly placed as well," she said. "How can we be so far off, then?"

Cameron leaned in toward his monitor. He was busy doing engineering formulas on his phone. He tried calculating the distance from Juana's position to Maria Elena's, cross-checking that with the platform's mounting brackets. He became stumped himself. Then, he shivered.

"*Archimedes*, how are we looking?" Juana asked. "Power on each submersible is getting low if we still want to mount and seal."

"We're working, Cameron needs a minute to figure it out." Maria Elena turned to the engineer in the submersible with her. "Cameron, you cold? That's not like you."

"I know, I should've listened to you," Cameron said.

"I know you should have – why do you think I wear this jacket? It gets cold as shit down here," Maria Elena stopped. She pulled up the temperature gauge.

"That phrase never made sense to me, 'cold as shit.' Shit's pretty warm. Same with 'cold as hell.' Isn't hell supposed to be fire and brimstone and…"

"Cameron, hang on. Sorry." Maria Elena looked at the temperature. "What did we calculate for cold compression?"

"How do you mean?" Cameron asked.

"I mean, when the manufacturer made the panels, how much did they calculate for compression when the metal got cold?" Maria Elena asked.

"We made sure to account for depth, forty-eight degrees Fahrenheit," Cameron said. "Plus, it can withstand freezing temperatures."

"We're reading forty-one right now," Maria Elena said. "Just because it can withstand freezing temps, doesn't mean it won't compress more."

"Because the temperature readings were taken late summer," Cameron replied. "Shit."

"Okay," Maria Elena paused. "Okay. We've got ninety-six minutes of battery."

"All right." Cameron wiped his dry erase board empty. "You said five-six centimeters before the rod can enter the mount, right?"

"Yup," she replied.

Cameron drew a figure on his board. He worked on figuring out the problem while Maria Elena grabbed the radio. "*Anaximander*, this is the *Archimedes*. Temperature compression measurements were taken in late summer, we're seven degrees cooler. May have been manufacturing error by a centimeter or two with the mounting bracket placements, but we're also likely dealing with the metal compressing. With such a large panel, it added up."

"So, what's the solve?" Juana asked.

"Cameron's working on it," Maria Elena responded. She put the radio down, then looked at the small dry erase board as he drew some numbers. "What are you trying to figure out?"

He put in his last number, accenting it by tapping his cell phone with extra pressure and frustration. "It's too far. We obviously can't alter the compression, so what are our options? Retract the panel, get teams to the docks to change the mounting brackets on everything..."

Cameron waited. Maria Elena thought about the options for a moment. "Move the concrete bases."

"And based on the power capabilities of the submersible, I think we can mount three of the four corners, then drag the fourth six centimeters and we're good to go," Cameron said.

"That kind of drag is going to exhaust the power supply," Maria Elena said. "So, we'll have to act fast."

She radioed the plan to the team. The *Boundless* lowered the north-facing half, placing the mounting brackets for the *Anaximander* and *Plutarch* without any issue. The crane brought the southeast corner down for the *Proclus*. The concrete base rod scraped against the mounting bracket but was still placed. When the final crane brought Maria Elena's corner down for the *Archimedes,* the rod rested on the edge of the mounting bracket, with just under half of the rod on the inside, the rest against the metal panel.

"How's your battery?" Cameron asked.

"Thirty-four percent," Maria Elena replied. "Just under an hour."

"Okay," Cameron said. "One thing I didn't think about."

"What's that?" she asked.

"How are we moving the base?" Cameron asked.

Maria Elena looked at the concrete below the rod, four wide, but equal sides to provide a strong support to rest the station on. Each side also had a handle to hook. The handles were installed to use the crane system on the *Boundless* to lower them to the ocean floor. But now, she saw an ulterior purpose for the handles. "Release the hooks on the three mounted sides and attach them to the base hooks from when we lowered them in the first place. Have three submersibles pull. The energy from all three will surely be sufficient to move it enough."

"Sounds good to me," Cameron said.

"Hey, *Anaximander*, we've got a plan. Have the *Boundless* release harnesses from the three bases we've attached to, we mount them on the concrete base over here on my end, then we pull those straps. We'll be pulling by the base so risk of tipping is minimal. One sub per harness," Maria Elena explained. "Then have the *Boundless* pull this side up slightly so we don't have to deal with the extra weight."

"You think that'll work?" Juana asked.

"It's the best idea I have for all of us running on what's about an hour's worth of battery or less," she replied.

"All right. No risk of damage to anything, right?" her older sister asked.

"It's a metal rod in concrete going into a metal panel meant to withstand the Pacific Ocean – we can beat these things up a little," Maria Elena replied.

"Okay, hell with it. *Boundless*, we're unhooking the three mounted sides. But do not retract the harnesses. In fact, please give us twenty-five meters of slack on the north-side harnesses and fifteen on the southeast," Juana radioed. "*Archimedes*, you came up with the idea and you've got one of our engineers in there with you. Why don't you take the lead?"

"Are you sure?" Maria Elena asked.

"You've got this, sis," she replied. "Plus, if it goes to hell, I won't have to take the blame."

"Smart ass," Maria Elena said. "All right, *Anaximander*, *Proclus*, and *Plutarch*, head up topside, unhook and bring your harnesses over."

The spotlights of the submersibles disappeared from view as Maria Elena remained under the panel. The loud, but muffled sound of the slack falling on the topside and coiling on to the panel rippled from above. Maria Elena moved her submersible around the bottom to the west side, the only one they didn't have to strap a harness to. They'd have to push the bracket northeast to get the rod into the mounting bracket.

The spotlight of the *Proclus* shone over the edge of the panel. The submersible came over the top, floating down with the harness in one of the claws.

"*Proclus*, come on over to the south side of the base and link up your harness to it," Maria Elena said. "*Archimedes, Plutarch*, when you get here, link up to the north and east side hooks on the concrete base, respectively."

The three other submersibles made their way to her, harnesses in tow. The elongated straps bowed from the current as it pulled them back. The submersible drivers connected their hooks to the concrete base one at a time. Each connection sent an echoing clank through the water.

"Okay, *Boundless*, make sure your one harness stays tight. Don't want the panel dropping like a ton of bricks once we're lined up," Maria Elena radioed. "All submersibles move on my signal. Pull on 'go.'"

Maria Elena lined her submersible up with the large concrete base, putting the front of the machine against it.

"What are you doing?" Cameron asked.

"Pushing," she replied. "The sub can take pressure over three times more intense than where we're at, a little nudge against some concrete won't hurt it."

A thud let out from the submersible against the concrete. Maria Elena turned her attention to the radio.

"Here we go," she said.

"Go?" Kit asked inside the *Plutarch*.

"No, I meant, 'here we go,' as in let's get started, then I'd do a countdown," Maria Elena replied. "Sorry. Okay, are we good to get started?"

"Good to go," Kit replied.

"Now we're going?" Ateera asked.

"No, everyone stop saying the word 'go.' Let me count us down," Maria Elena demanded. "Three, two, and one. Go."

All four submersibles kicked their engines into full gear. Silt and sand stirred up, most of it sent directly at the *Archimedes*, the natural flow of the current pushing the agitated surface her way.

The base didn't move. The engines on the submersibles whirred in a strain, the harnesses taut and unmoving from the increase in tension. The hooks connected to the base groaned against the increase in pressure.

"Come on, we only need a few centimeters," Maria Elena said.

Her jaw clenched, the muscles below her cheeks tightening. She stopped pushing and backed her submersible up.

"Are we stopping?" Juana asked.

"No, keep pulling," Maria Elena said. "But move up as well, try pulling back and up simultaneously, see if we can relieve the weight a bit."

"Makes sense," Juana said. "What are you doing?"

"Giving you a push," she replied.

"No, you are not," Juana said.

Maria Elena moved the submersible back.

"Wait, are we going to ram concrete?" Cameron asked.

"No, 'ram' is much too violent. I prefer 'nudge.'" Maria Elena lined the side of the submersible up with the base. "The left side has the least vital equipment, plus a good portion of the hull isn't the viewport. We'll be fine."

"I don't know – we're using a submersible to ram a huge slab of concrete at the bottom of the Pacific," Cameron said. "You don't see a problem with that?"

"Nah." Maria Elena waved him off. "I've gone into rock faces going twice as fast as we'll hit. And stop saying 'ram.' We're not ramming into it, we're nudging."

"Oh, nudging the concrete base with our submersible at the bottom of the Pacific, how silly of me." Cameron sat back in his chair, folding his arms and waiting for the event to unfold.

"Coming in," Maria Elena radioed.

The submersible moved toward the base, left side facing the concrete. The adjustable engines allowed for her to steer the sub in any direction Maria Elena pleased.

"*Archimedes*, back off," Juana radioed. "We'll find another way."

Maria Elena picked up speed as the submersible moved closer to the base. She made quick alterations to make it as flush with the base as possible, inching it forward to have the majority of the impact be received on the metal hull at the back side.

"Maria Elena," Juana said.

The *Archimedes* hit. The base moved. A fresh wave of debris and silt stirred up from the base, covering the area as it swirled about in a small storm.

"Okay, stop," Maria Elena radioed.

"How's the hull?" Cameron asked.

"Doing just fine, told you it would be," she responded. "There'll be some scratches and dings. Just giving it some character."

"What the hell were you thinking?" Juana asked.

Maria Elena ignored her older sister, instead checking the alignment. After a moment, she hopped on the radio. "*Boundless*, this is the *Archimedes*. Give us a minute to unhook the harnesses and move out of the way, then you are clear to lower the panel."

"What?" Juana radioed.

"Check it, the nudge got us exactly where we needed it to be," Maria Elena said.

The radio went silent for a while. Finally, Juana was back. "Our batteries are getting too low to argue about this here. All submersibles detach your harnesses from the base."

They did, after moving away from the base and the panel. They waited for the *Boundless* to lower the panel. Minutes later, the panel slid into place with ease. The rod entered the mounting bracket perfectly.

Maria Elena piloted the *Archimedes* over the top of the panel, unhooking the final harness as the panel rested perfectly in place. She backed the submersible up, pulled out her phone and activated her camera.

"What're you doing?" Cameron asked.

"Taking a picture, I want to remember this," she answered.

"We'll tighten the brackets later. Let's get the remaining panels aligned first over the next few days – that way if we have to adjust, we'll have the wiggle room," Juana said. "All submersibles return to the surface. Space out a minimum of ten meters for the ascent."

The radio remained quiet for most of the journey up. The *Boundless* requested estimated damage to the *Archimedes*, and Maria Elena replied it was cosmetic only. Juana insisted on a full system check when they arrived back on the deck of the main ship.

At the surface, their submersibles were brought up one by one by a huge crane. As Maria Elena stepped out of the *Archimedes*, she caught her sister shooting toward her like an arrow. Maria Elena went down the last rungs, stepping on to the boat surface. Her older sister didn't wait for her to turn around and face her before tearing into her.

"This isn't just about you, you know?" Juana said.

"I know, it was about all of us running out of power and time." Maria Elena turned. She grabbed the cable from the charging station, pulling up a panel on the back to plug into the *Archimedes*. "What were we going to do? Leave the panel unconnected and hanging there?"

"We had three of the brackets mounted, it would've been completely fine," Juana responded. "It would've been safer than you using your sub like a battering ram."

"Oh, my god," Maria Elena said. "I didn't ram anything. I nudged the damned thing. You put me in charge, you wanted a solution, the panel is in place. The sub is barely dinged up."

Maria Elena did, however, ram the charging cable into the socket on the *Archimedes*. She pulled it out and pushed it back in again when the charge didn't start the first try.

"After you risked Cameron, and all of our safety," Juana said.

"All of us?" Maria Elena said, letting the panel go, hitting the top of the charging cable.

Cameron tried to interject but left them alone after a few tries.

"What if you breached? We would've had to have scrambled to rescue you," Juana said.

"That's an exaggeration," Maria Elena said. "The sub is fine."

Donnie had stepped out of the control room of the *Boundless*. He approached the group, waving his hands in the air. "Whoa, whoa, hey. I get it. I get what's happening here, but it doesn't have to."

"The shit it doesn't," Juana said. "What she did was reckless."

"You and I have been upended and shot against coral and rocks in a submersible, so you know the subs can take it," Maria Elena argued.

"We didn't choose to get upended, nature did that to us. So, while we were fine it wasn't our choice to make. Today, you made the choice to create that danger," Juana said. "I can't always be here to help you, Maria Elena."

"Fine, we'll do something different for the rest," Maria Elena said. "Would love to hear what everyone thinks that'll be." They all went silent for a moment, soaking in that they had to adjust more bases. "Yeah, we've got five more panels, and unless they were made completely differently, we've got this problem ahead of us with every single one for the next five days. We've got panel loading times at night, so we can't send the *Boundless*. We're already on a twenty-four-hour rotation."

"Alright, that's enough," Donnie said. "Let's push our next panel back a day, give our engineers some time to figure out a solution and get more exact calculations. That way we can avoid any further problems or risks. Okay?"

Juana and Maria Elena nodded, saying nothing more.

"This crew, you guys are killing me," Donnie said, walking back toward the control room.

The *Boundless* turned slowly, lumbering toward the shore, which was nowhere in sight yet. Most of the crew ate their dinner inside. Maria Elena sat on the deck, legs crossed, eating in silence as she looked out at the water. Cameron approached her, his own plate loaded with chicken and vegetables.

"Can I join you?" he asked.

"You're not mad at me?" Maria Elena looked up at him.

Cameron groaned as he sat on the deck next to her. "No, I'm not mad at you. You scared the shit out of me, but I never doubted you."

"Good to know," Maria Elena asked.

"I would've said something, but I had to let the two of you play that argument out." Cameron took a bite of his chicken. "I've got three daughters, two of them teenagers. I know when to step in and when it's best to let siblings get through it. You were both trying to protect something."

Maria Elena kept her composure. It didn't stop a tear falling from her eyes. "Yeah, what's that?"

"You were protecting your decision, because you are stubborn and daring as hell, but you also knew you were right." Cameron swallowed his chicken.

"What about my older sister?" She wiped the tear, then grabbed some fries and dipped them in ketchup. "Isn't she supposed to have my back? Protect me?"

"She was protecting you," Cameron said. "I know she said you endangered everyone, but then she talked about how she couldn't always be there to help you. She didn't mean everyone, we were all fine. You are her 'everyone.' She cares too damned much about you, I know. I can see it."

"Yeah." Maria Elena chewed her fries. Neither cared about manners, they could eat and talk in front of one another. "And that line about not being able to help me… I think she's leaving. Taking another job after this one is done."

"Really?" Cameron replied.

She nodded. "She's wanted to for a long time. We just haven't been able to find a way to say goodbye yet."

"Well, just because someone leaves, doesn't mean a relationship has to change. She'll always be your sister." Cameron took another bite of chicken. "Your family is your blood, and that doesn't leave you."

"Unless somebody guts you, then blood leaves." Maria Elena chewed thoughtfully.

"Good lord," Cameron said.

"Kidding, morbidly." She smiled. "Thanks, Cameron."

"You're welcome. Hey, I grabbed my usual post-workout meal, but I haven't lifted today. You want any of this?" Cameron asked, gesturing to his plate.

"Get that healthy shit away from me." Maria Elena wiped away another tear. "Can't you see I'm eating my feelings?"

"Sorry," Cameron said.

"Seriously, I've never seen you eat garbage. I get you love staying in shape, but seriously, do you ever cheat on your meal plan?"

"Oh, I do," Cameron said. "Tell you what, next cheat day, let's go to a diner."

"Get a number eight?" Maria Elena said.

"Octopus' breakfasts for both of us," Cameron replied. He took a large forkful of vegetables, shoving them further up the fork as he added a piece of chicken and took the entire bite at once.

"Hey, wanted to show you something." Maria Elena leaned to her left. She reached into her jean pocket to get her cell phone.

"Oh, yeah, I saw you taking pictures of the panel," Cameron said.

She nodded. Pulling up her photos, Maria Elena scanned through the ones she took for the right one. Once she found the one with the perfect angle, she moved in closer toward Cameron.

"The light caught the name perfectly." Maria Elena zoomed in.

"Wow, I saw the name on the panel before we dove, but there in the water," Cameron paused. "That's so cool."

Maria Elena took one last look. In the photo, the spotlights of the *Archimedes* submersible shone on the silver panel they had put in place that day. The illumination hit right near the base where the mounting bracket was. On the panel were five letters, long and sleek, the station's name: *Thales*.

DAYS TO LAUNCH: 644

The *Anaximander* lifted out of the Pacific, hoisted by the crane toward the *Boundless*. Juana sat beside Cody; on the outside, gallons of water poured off the rounded glass viewport in front, and around them. The world came into clearer view with each passing moment, water splashing back into the ocean below.

Juana sighed, unable to do anything until they reached the ship's main deck. As she waited, she sat back in her chair, tilting her head back and closing her eyes.

"Doing okay over there, chief?" Cody asked.

"Yeah, will be. Glad this stint is over," Juana said. "Those extra days from the realignments really added up."

"No kidding," Cody said. "We still haven't fine-tuned the mounting brackets or performed the final seal on the panel edges. That puts us, what? Five days behind already."

"Yup." Juana kept her eyes closed, head back.

What exhausted her more were the inner desires and voices speaking to her. She wanted to get away, the monotony had settled in and she was tired of a stagnant life. It showed in a few mistakes, unwilling laziness taking hold. Juana didn't mean to cause complications, but as her heart drifted further from the project, she found herself inadvertently less invested. A loose strand of her black hair had come out of her ponytail. She pinched it with her fingers, twirling it in a rhythm as they waited to get aboard the *Boundless*.

The submersible base touched down on the *Boundless'* surface. Juana stayed in her chair, sighing again before flipping switches to shut down all of the systems and engines.

"Want me to plug in the charger?" Cody asked.

She nodded. "That'd be great, thanks."

"You sure you're okay?" he asked.

"I will be. Just need to get some rest, stop making those mistakes." Juana stood. She made her way up the ladder for the access hatch.

"You're only human. How many trips have we made where nothing went wrong?" Cody asked.

"Yeah, but I knew if I put too much pressure on the bolt, it'd snap. The cold only makes it more sensitive, shouldn't have over torqued it." Juana said. "Otherwise we'd only be four days behind."

"It's one bolt," Cody said. "World's not blowing up."

"It's burning, though, and in need of us powering up to help the west coast." Juana opened the door overhead. A few light drips of water came through as the sunlight shone through the opened hatch. Juana tilted her head down, letting the drips of water hit her neck and back. She climbed out and onto the deck.

"Hey!" Cody shouted, as he often did. "Don't be so hard on yourself. You're doing your best and literally no one can do what you can because no one ever has, okay?"

"Okay, thanks, *jefe*!" Juana pointed one thumb up in the air as she walked away. "Thanks for plugging him in, too."

"We're pioneers in uncharted space, Juana," Cody said. He threw up his arms in celebration, pumping his fist like a wide receiver showing off after a touchdown, the submersible charger cable in hand. The cable itself flailed about as he rejoiced. "God damned pioneers!"

She smirked at his victory dance. Cody's large belly jiggled as he pumped his fist one more time. Juana entered the ship, looking for Donnie or Jason. They weren't on the captain's deck where they normally sat during the excursions down to the ocean bottom. She passed Paxton, the radio operator for the *Boundless*.

"Hey, Paxton," Juana said. "Where are they?"

"Not sure, they left the main deck pretty much once you started your ascent," Paxton replied.

Her brow scrunched. "Huh, thanks."

Juana walked through a long hall toward the restroom, taking a quick break before looking around for them. As she opened the door, she overheard an argument echoing from down the hall. She took a step into the restroom, stopping once she recognized the heightened voices. It was Donnie and Jason. She couldn't make out what was being said, only that they seemed at odds with one another, not something she was accustomed to. They gave each other grief, yes, but this was the first time she'd ever heard them flat out shouting at one another.

She stepped into the restroom, deciding it wasn't her business. They were honest with the crew, so anything she and the rest had to know, she trusted Donnie and Jason to divulge it, if it was even related to them. Hopping out of the restroom a few minutes later, the space down the hall was silent. Completely silent. Juana stood at the end of the hall, unsure if she should walk down to check or not.

91

The sound of frenetic work on the outside deck made its way into the hall, the only sound in the corridor for a time. The silence was broken by Jason clearing his throat. She took one step toward the exit but turned around, headed back toward Donnie and Jason.

"Take care of one more person instead of yourself, Juana," she muttered to herself quietly while shaking her head.

Juana stepped heavily, trying to alert them she was coming. She knocked on the doorframe before entering, as one more added precaution.

"Um, yeah, come on in," Donnie said.

Inside the room, Donnie tipped his Styrofoam cup to get one last sip of coffee. Both he and Jason leaned over their laptops. Donnie's hair was tousled in an uncontrolled manor.

"Hey guys," Juana said.

"Hey, Juana, what's up?" Jason asked, folding away his laptop and focusing on his crewmember.

"Had a request to run by you, if that's okay," she said.

"Go for it." Jason looked over at Donnie, waiting for his partner to acknowledge Juana. "Donnie."

Donnie had one hand in his hair, fingers pulling at the strands, while the other scrolled across his screen.

"Donnie!" Jason said firmly.

Donnie dropped his hand from his hair to the table. He shot up, seeing Juana for the first time. "Hey Juana, what's up?"

"She has a request for us," Jason said. "So maybe let's give her our attention, rather than fish through more code."

"Yup," Donnie said. He tried taking a sip from his Styrofoam cup, getting nothing. "I need more coffee. Want to walk and talk?"

Juana nodded. Jason and Donnie stood. The three of them made their way to the kitchen and dining space.

"They have Styrofoam cups?" Juana asked.

"I know, right?" Donnie replied. "Here we are, trying to create the cleanest, most powerful energy station the world has ever seen, and we can't invest in some biodegradable or reusable cups."

"What's the request, Juana?" Jason spoke over Donnie.

They entered the dining hall. Two coffee carafes sat on a table. Donnie tried the first carafe, which was empty.

"So, I know we just did a lot of extra days to make up for the lost time because of the cold impacting the panels – all those adjustments set us back a bit," Juana said.

Donnie tried the second carafe, pouring coffee.

"Anyway," Juana continued. "Was wondering whether we can space out the workdays if we run into similar issues going forward. At least get one day a week off."

The carafe sputtered its last liquid, giving just enough for Donnie to fill his cup. He opened the carafe top to make another batch.

"Yeah," Jason said. "We didn't really put in any kind of labor information regarding snags like this, did we?"

Donnie looked around for filters, opening cabinet after cabinet, looking up and down.

"No, we didn't. And this crew is great, but I fear we could work ourselves too hard if we don't set some kind of limits," Juana said. "We have so many snags like this coming our way, and I know you're under pressure because old energy prices are out of control. This station has so much riding on it. And we're all here to get the work done."

"But if we lose every weekend and free day by making up for problems, we'll drive you all into the ground," Jason said.

"Exactly," Juana replied.

"Wasn't our intention, believe me," Jason said. "Donnie and I can talk to the engineering department, see if we can get ahead of some of the added labor we didn't calculate for."

"That'd be nice." Juana looked at Donnie, wondering if she could help him find the filters. "There are just so many factors once we're down there, it ends up taking more time than we want, but at the same time it's not like we can afford to mess this up."

"Absolutely. What started as an idea of how to change energy use in the states became a necessity real fast. When Donnie and I started, we just wanted to improve clean energy use, we did not want this project to become the west coast's economic salvation. We'll make sure we're taking care of the ones taking care of this project," Jason said. He stared at Donnie, who whispered under his breath. "Right, Donnie?"

"Huh?" Donnie's eyes went wide and his face like a student called on by the teacher when he had no real answer prepared. "Yeah, absolutely."

He went right back to rifling through cabinets, looking for something.

"Okay, thanks. I'm happy to help with giving some insight into potential snags we may encounter. I see loading having some definite complications, too. It's not just the dive crew," Juana said.

"Absolutely, send us what you're thinking, we'll make sure those are brought up so we can plan accordingly," Jason said. "Donnie, what are you looking for?"

"Filters, seriously, how is this such a problem?" Donnie asked.

"It may not be." Jason leaned down and opened the bottom left cabinet. When he didn't see them immediately, he shuffled the large stack of napkins around, and there they were. "They were right there, Donnie. No problem existed."

"Okay, thanks," Donnie replied. "Except the problem was what we couldn't see. The solution was there, but there was other stuff in the way."

Juana helped him with the coffee grounds. Donnie shut the lid and got a new carafe going.

"You sure you're okay?" Juana asked.

"Yeah." Donnie activated the brew. The drip into the carafe started as he took in a massive breath and let out a huge sigh. "Yeah, just working through some stuff. And it's probably nothing."

"Okay, but you promise me if it is something, you'll tell me?" Juana asked.

"Sure, thank you, Juana," Donnie said. "Sorry for being so absentminded. We've got a lot going on and we're trying to help."

"I know," Juana said. "You guys are great. You support the crew, but you're also under a huge amount of pressure. Plus, we all feel a need to deliver the best, so help us out to make sure we're at our best. It's showing."

"Thanks, Juana," Jason said. "Was that everything?"

She almost told them about her upcoming departure but because it was so far away, it wasn't the time. "Nah, that was it. You guys have a good rest of your day."

Juana left, letting them resume their conversation from before, but with quiet and calm demeanors this time. She could hear a few quick exchanges as she left.

"We'll keep an eye open, okay?" Jason negotiated with Donnie. "If we see any signs, we'll raise the flag."

"Something just seemed off," Donnie said.

After that, their voices became indiscernible again. She wondered what seemed off but couldn't do anything about it for the moment. She had to trust the ones who hired her, the ones who fought to make the *Thales* reality.

DAYS TO LAUNCH: 6

The newly promoted Director of Operations, Yuki Sanada, grew increasingly nervous as his crew enjoyed the lavish party thrown by Maritimus Energy. Such a lack of focus the night before the final dive was not something Yuki took lightly, particularly with one new recruit whose diving experience ended with snorkel gear. The crew had also taken hardly any time off since losing two of their own only a few months ago. However, the executives and higher powers at Maritimus Energy wanted the extravagant night with the entire crew, new recruits, and traumatized veterans alike on hand.

Yuki, an aged former Naval captain, stood on the outside of the party. His role throughout the night left him feeling more excluded as time went on. He thought he was giving a speech at the party, but the agenda left time only for executives and politicians. He wanted nothing more than to find the exit. As he eyed the door out, he heard Cody flag down a server, making sure he tried every appetizer and ocean-themed drink the event had to offer.

Ewan and Stacey, the other two new recruits, walked toward Yuki with bright blue drinks in hand. Ewan stood over six feet tall, something he and Cameron shared. Maria Elena not far behind, pushing six feet herself. Stacey was fair-skinned with dark, auburn hair. Her wide smile and bright eyes accentuated her dedicated spirit. He was very happy about the two latest additions to the crew. Stacey's presence as a former Coast Guard nurse brought much-needed comfort to the others. Eric helped with his renewable energy expertise. They couldn't replace the lost crew members, but they filled vital spots and would hopefully give a renewed sense of purpose.

As they made their way through the crowd, navigating with martini glasses filled to the brim, Yuki found himself distracted by the large venue's elaborate decorations. Hanging above the crowd of politicians, lobbyists, executives, and other people of power and influence were flowing pieces of light blue fabric. The fabric spun in circles as lights moved frenetically around the cloth, a simulation of the ocean current they were harnessing. All of the spinning pieces moved toward one of the turbines, the centerpiece of the ceiling's decorations. The turbine was huge, even in the high vaulted facility. The circular white shell was hoisted and held by a series of vast, metallic supports. They had removed two sets of blades from the turbine, leaving only one set out of three to avoid the fixture taking over the entire ceiling. Yuki smiled, greeting Eric and Stacey as they nudged past a man wearing a partially unbuttoned silk shirt who was oblivious to their existence.

"What's so funny, sir?" Stacey asked, leaning in and tilting her ear toward him to hear over the music.

"Oh, nothing," Yuki smirked, pointing at the ceiling. "Feels like they should have people on the turbine dancing on the blades or something. Seems kind of wasteful for a party about saving the planet with renewable energy."

"I know, it's pretty crazy," Stacey replied, smiling. "Here, I got you an Ocean Mist Martini, Mr. Sanada."

He cringed. "Please, call me Yuki. I don't need a reminder of how old I am."

She nodded her head in agreement, then raised her martini. The glasses clinked. Yuki stared at his beverage while Eric and Stacey sipped from theirs. Yuki took a quick sip, cringing from the taste. Stacey looked at him and her young face wrinkled. "Do you not like it? I could get you something else."

"No, don't worry about it, I was just thinking to myself," Yuki hesitated, leaning in closer so they could actually hear one another. He nearly told her how long it'd been since he'd taken a drink, but Yuki could tell Stacey was one who prided herself on helping others and stopped. "Are you two feeling comfortable about the dive tomorrow?"

"I'm a little nervous," Eric replied.

He really meant "nervous as hell," Yuki could sense as much. It was the same innocence and anticipation in young faces from his days in the Navy. Yuki turned toward Eric to reassure him. "Don't worry about it. Maria Elena is amazing. It's just over an hour from the start of the dive to stepping up that ladder into the *Thales*. We've got a great crew you're joining. The six of them have worked on the station for over a year, if not more."

A few tables away, Karina and Flannery sipped gin martinis. Stacey smiled and waved at the two. Yuki and Eric took up vacant seats outside of the main party. The new recruit's gaze was far off; whatever he was thinking about, it certainly wasn't the present. A loud ruckus grew closer.

"And here come the Core Four," Yuki said.

"It's Juana, Maria Elena, Cameron, and Cody, right?" Stacey clarified.

"You got it."

The four headed toward them, but it was proving a long trip through the sea of bodies crowding the bar area.

"Hey, Stacey, I was thinking about it and I may have you train on some basic stuff with different jobs because I have a feeling you're the one who's going to need some extracurricular activities," Yuki said. "At least as our nurse, I hope you do. You're the only crew member whose skillsets I would prefer not to use."

"I was thinking the same. That'd be great," she smiled. She had clearly predicted the same level of boredom headed her way.

"Cameron and Cody could teach you the mechanical engineering stuff. Juana or Maria Elena may even take you out in the submersibles once in a while, see how the turbines work. It's a blast." Yuki smiled as he continued, "I hope you packed a couple of books you can read."

"I have, I actually am reading one right now…"

Her sentence went unfinished as the four reached the group. Cameron towered over everyone, even the alarmingly tall Maria Elena. Yuki and Cameron went back several years as Yuki had commanded Cameron on a submarine when he was just a kid – now the aging man was a single, African American father of three. The Core Four homed in on Stacey, but made sure to include Eric, who was the most introverted among the team thus far.

"What is this little drink you have?" Cody asked.

"It's an Ocean Mist martini, Karina suggested it," Stacey replied.

"That is absurd. We're getting a shot for you right now. Eric, you're jumping in on this with us," Cody shouted.

Eric did such a subtle nod even the observant Yuki had a hard time seeing if it was a yes or no. Cody worked on gaining the attention of the bartender. Yuki secretly wasn't looking forward to being in the *Thales* with Cody. He was a clever kid, but his volume level had no filter and his love of a chaotic lifestyle had the potential to become troublesome. There was always one comedian that seemed harmless but led to accidents. Yuki was too early into his job to know for sure if that was the case, but his exuberant behavior and attempts for distraction made him nervous.

"Hey, buddy. Champ. Tiger!" Cody tried different approaches to get the bartender's attention. "All right, Stacey, get up here, you've got that smile. Work it."

Stacey blushed and Yuki could already see it happening. Cody was both very smart and very dumb. He was flirting with a crewmember, something he absolutely shouldn't do. Yet he knew the exact tactic to make her feel empowered; the bartender was over there in a matter of seconds. The Core Four, as the crew had come to refer to the first recruits, cheered her on while Eric smiled.

"Um, we need a few drinks," Stacey said.

"What'll you have?"

"We need some shots," Cody added. "I'm thinking tequila – that won't make me regret my life in the morning."

"I'm sorry, sir, the selection tonight is limited to our ocean themed drinks for the event."

"Okay, then, give us a Wave Crash," Cody fired back in an instant.

"I'm not familiar, sir," the bartender said.

"Oh, it's real simple, equal parts vodka and Blue Curacao. Seven shots, please, good sir."

"Six, Cody," Yuki chimed in.

"Come on, captain, it's our last night before we're headed down," Cody said, shrugging in disappointment that he couldn't corrupt his leader. "And only six days to launch!"

"Exactly, we dive tomorrow and I'm in Juana's submersible on the first dive with you, Cody. If you puke in that thing, you're cleaning the entire *Anaximander* with your toothbrush," Yuki said.

"You've got nothing to worry about, sir," Cody continued. "You've got the biggest crew ever! A fat guy, an Irish girl, and three at least six feet tall! We can handle the booze. Stacey and Karina are the only one you have to worry about."

The older sister to the entire world around her, Juana slapped Cody on the arm. "You are not fat. Stop making those kind of jokes about yourself."

The two compared their stomachs, Cody clearly winning with his prominent gut.

"See? Look at that!" Cody shouted.

"You're just a big boy, now where's my drink?" Juana asked.

He turned around, grabbing the tray of shots. They raised their glasses in the air. Yuki excused himself and made his way toward Karina and Flannery. When he passed by an empty table, he calmly put his martini glass on it, leaving it behind before reaching the duo.

"Hey guys, they should be starting in about ten minutes," he said.

"Sounds good, sir," Karina said. "Thanks."

Yuki couldn't believe most of them still called him sir. He was retired from the military and hated the formality. However, if it meant they viewed him as a leader, he wouldn't fight it. The former executive and programmer were both doing much better with their drinking, indulging but nowhere close to excess.

"What are you drinking?" Yuki asked.

"We've got Clear Water martinis," Karina said. She rotated her ankles with uncomfortable heels on. "Fancy name for a straight martini. What about you?"

"Oh, I don't drink much, but I might if Flannery ordered me some good whiskey," Yuki said. "Surprised you're not drinking some now."

"As much as I want to refute your assumptions about my Irish-as-hell last name, I do drink whiskey. I'll get you one later and bring it to you," Flannery answered.

"Thanks, have them put it on the rocks. Can't handle neat in my older age." Yuki checked his cell phone and brought up his messages. He hadn't received any notifications, but it didn't stop him from checking the text chain he had with his daughter. Nothing from her.

Meanwhile, the sound of Cody's voice traveled across the open floor congested with strangers.

"Shall we join them?" Flannery asked as she and Karina made their way toward them and urged Yuki to come with them.

As quickly as he tried to get away from it all, he put his phone away and walked with the two. Everyone celebrated the whole crew coming together. Karina whispered to Stacey, who nodded toward Cody. Yuki smiled; Karina had likely warned her ahead of time about what to expect from the chubby comedian.

The lights faded to an absurd level of darkness, the only illumination coming from above where the torches recreating the ocean stayed lit. The atmosphere of near pitch black was a much better representation of what it was like down in the *Thales* than any of the flashy decorations he'd seen thus far. The spotlights came up. Senators, representatives, labor union reps, the stage was full of expensive suits, everyone dressed almost the same. Dr. Scott, the designer who helped Cody and Cameron with the original turbines, sat in one of the prominent seats. His assistant was on the stage beginning the festivities. Yuki turned from the stage to his crew.

"Sir, they're starting," Juana stated. "Should we go up there?"

"I'm staying here," Yuki said.

"You should be up there. You're our new boss for this whole thing, our 'captain.' What about your speech?" Maria Elena asked.

"I'm not giving one," he responded.

The crew went silent. Their captain wasn't giving a speech to his own crew the night before departure.

"Ocean Wave Crash, sir?" Cody asked.

"What the hell is that?" Yuki asked. "I don't care what it is, sure. No, on second thought, Flannery, I'll go ahead and take you up on that whiskey."

As Dr. Scott finished his introduction, a familiar song came on and everyone groaned. "Firing Comets," the uplifting ballad about fixing the world, played any time promotional material for Maritimus Energy, or the *Thales*, was used.

"Wow, you weren't kidding, Maria Elena," Eric continued. "They really do play this song with anything regarding the *Thales*, that's three times in less than two hours. Talk about over-saturating your marketing."

"We started taking bets on how many times in a day we hear 'Firing Comets.' What did everyone put in for this? I'm at eight," Maria Elena said.

"Seven," Cody said.

"Five," Cameron said.

"Nine," Juana said.

"Wow, could I put twenty dollars on six?" Eric asked.

"No, you may not," Karina stopped him.

"Is that your guess?" Eric replied.

"You know it," Karina smiled. "There are still open bets on four or eleven, though."

"No way it'll be four. Eleven it is," Eric said.

As the soft narration from the video came to a close, the song, "Firing Comets," came back into focus during the "making progress montage", as Flannery called it. The song was saturated in overly corny lyrics about healing the world, everyone "firing comets to heal the sky, firing comets to heal the waters." Basically, the lyrics talked about firing a lot of comets to heal a lot of things. The Core Four continued to work on their harmonies as they mocked the unintentionally hilarious song aimed at the most devoted of democratic idealists. The applause from the crowd of lobbyists, executives, and other people in roles of importance could not have been more on cue as the video finished. The corporate and political figures had clearly been to so many of these functions, they had their methods and practices down to near perfection. Senator Matthew McCreary stepped up to the podium.

"Thank you all, ladies and gentlemen, for coming," Matthew cleared his throat. "At this time, we would like to acknowledge the amazing crew that will be diving over two thousand eight hundred feet below the surface of the Pacific Ocean tomorrow. They are the crew of the *Thales* station and will be the first ones to allow the west coast of the country to see the first true sign of economic hope and recovery in several months, perhaps years. Ladies and gentlemen, I give you the crew of the *Thales*."

Everyone applauded as Matthew looked to a vacant set of chairs. Yuki scratched his chin and turned toward the bar, embarrassed.

"You didn't know they were doing that, did you, sir?" Cameron asked.

"No, I most certainly did not," Yuki said quickly.

Taking the hit for the team, Cameron gestured to Matthew, trying to give away their location. It would have worked had Matthew been looking. Yuki grew frustrated as more time passed, people on the stage trying to tell him where they were. Finally, he caught wise and saw Yuki with his crew raising their glasses. Yuki figured Matthew was in his mid-thirties and full of dreams, young for a senator. He hadn't quite suffered the brutal truth of politics. He still believed politicians wouldn't drown in bureaucracy or get bought out by a lobbyist group with a lot of campaign donations at the ready.

"Ah, there they are. I do apologize," Matthew said.

"Sorry, Matty, we're just enjoying the open bar!" Cody exclaimed.

Almost everyone laughed. Yuki saw a few people in custom tailored suits and professional dresses remaining silent, showing their snooty disapproval of Cody daring to be so informal with a senator. Yuki found himself smiling, partnered with a simultaneous unease.

"Anyway, Captain Yuki Sanada will be the *Thales* Team Leader, acting as the Director of Operations. He's the older gentlemen… raising a shot glass," Matthew said.

The crew tried to keep from snickering. Matthew allowed a moment to pass where he clearly debated whether or not to continue.

"Our Energy Efficiency Consultant, Karina Trowbridge," Matthew said.

The crowd applauded, then stopped according to their high society training in delivering accolades. Yuki slipped back as the introductions continued, listening to the rounds of applause for each individual.

"Our Computer Systems Manager and Operator, Ava Flannery; Mechanical Specialist, Cameron Webb; Energy Systems Specialist, Cody Seacrest; Submersible Navigation Specialist, Maria Elena Perez; and Submersible Turbine Specialist, Juana Perez."

Yuki shook his head in disbelief, the list only reached seven. "You've got to be kidding me."

Matthew started rambling on about the accomplishments the crew would achieve, all to serve the financers and bureaucrats. An assistant came up and whispered to Matthew.

"I apologize, ladies and gentlemen. I forgot the two newest additions to the crew, Renewable Energy Analyst Eric Coleman and Medical Technician Stracey Fern."

Applause came from the crowd. The crew, however, looked apologetically back at their newest member, except for Cody, who shouted Stacey's name properly. The senator didn't notice. To their surprise, Stacey had burst out laughing.

"Sorry, Stacey," Cameron said.

"That's okay," Stacey said, laughing again.

"What's so funny?" Yuki asked.

"Stracey Fern? Seriously? Am I a registered nurse or a porn star?" she asked, now laughing uncontrollably.

"Stacey! Coming alive, I love it!" Cody shouted.

The speeches up front had a moment of disruption as the crew of the *Thales* laughed excessively, and a few who heard Cody were openmouthed in shock. Cody and Stacey gave one another a high five. They socialized while Matthew thanked an inordinate amount of people, feeding their status and ego. It was when things were wrapping up Cody looked at his leader and decided to take the moment and use it properly.

"All right, everyone," Cody lifted his glass. "Here's to Captain Yuki."

Everyone raised their drinks. In that moment, Yuki knew that he would never remember the union representative names or what organization made the rechargeable, lithium ion batteries for the deep-sea submersibles. What he would remember was the crew standing as one in support for one another.

"Do you want to give a speech?" Cody asked.

Yuki waved them off.

"No, come on," Stacey encouraged him, as did the rest of the crew.

Yuki smiled, trying to remain silent as the crew kept persisting.

"You can't let them take this away from you," Karina said.

Yuki's smile grew. "Okay, okay, okay."

The entire crew cheered. They raised their glasses to him. Cody squashed the celebration, insisting on waiting until Yuki gave his speech.

"Wait, let him go, then we can toast and shit," Cody said.

"Cody," Yuki scolded him.

"And stuff, sorry," he replied.

"Okay, tomorrow begins our journey to the bottom of the Pacific," Yuki said. "We know what's at stake if this station fails. Most of the west coast is waiting on us for this energy – with routine outages, soaring prices, they need an energy source that won't hurt the planet. There are so many reasons the world needs this station. But I want us to focus on our own, because what they really need is us. If we are safe and succeed, then that will permeate across the coast. For many of you, the danger is all too real. So, let's take care of each other, first and foremost."

Yuki raised his glass. The rest followed him. They took a sip.

"And let's take another drink for the two who started this all and the ones we lost." Yuki raised his glass. "To Donald Harmon, 'Donnie,' and Jason White."

"To Donnie and Jason," the crew said, as they raised their glasses.

"Let's keep each other safe, our success ensures their memory lives on," Yuki said.

The *Thales* crew raised their glasses to their two fallen members. As everyone at the party celebrated and congratulated one another, the crew quietly sipped from their glasses. The ones who conceived the idea of this station and would change the way the world thought about renewable energy, never got the chance to see their idea come to life.

DAYS TO LAUNCH: 5

Maria Elena sat behind the controls of the *Archimedes,* waiting for the green light to depart. Attached to the side bays of the station, the submersible rested underneath, sealed tight against a hatch that led to the *Thales.* Inside the sub, she grabbed a sticky note left by her sister on the dash. She left fun quotes behind for her. Juana always knew what she needed to hear, and the notes were her way of showing her love without saying it out loud. Pulling the sticky note from the dash, she read what Juana had left her.

Hardships often prepare ordinary people for an extraordinary destiny. C.S. Lewis

Maria Elena smirked.

"*Archimedes*, this is the *Thales*," Flannery radioed from the control room. "You are clear for departure. We'll begin with Grid B, work your way over."

"Copy that, *Archimedes* departing now," she replied.

Before placing the sticky note back on the dash of the submersible, she read it one more time, then slapped it near one of her camera monitors so she could easily see it. Maria Elena confirmed the hatches were closed for both the *Thales* and *Archimedes*, then threw the silver switch to release from the station.

The submersible detached from the station. Floating down, Maria Elena piloted the submersible to the right, out toward the kite fields where the turbines rested. The primary grids were still and wouldn't begin until the official launch. She navigated past row after row of stationary turbines. Each one was encased within a protective shell, the fronts and backs with grates to allow the water to easily pass through. Inside were three sets of three blades attached to a central rod. Every major grid had a thousand of those setups. Behind her was Grid Six. She coasted along Five, making her way toward Four. Grids One through Three were on the opposite side of the station. Within the pitch black, the turbine shells only became visible when her floodlights shone on them.

After passing the major grids, she reached the back of the station to Grid B, one of two smaller grids built to power the *Thales* and act as a backup. She stopped, hovering over the far-right corner of the turbines.

"Ready when you are," Maria Elena radioed.

"Hold tight," Flannery replied. "Configuring. Have to get power from both the temporary generator and the grid."

"How long after we activate these turbines will the station start to receive power?" Maria Elena asked.

"In theory, a matter of moments," Cameron chimed in.

"Cool," Maria Elena replied.

She looked out toward Grid Four, close to the back turbines where she waited for the go ahead. There was a dented spot in the sand between a few of the turbines, a spot left there by a sunken submersible she had to help retrieve.

"This is Yuki from the Shore Station. Everyone here says, 'thank you.' Me, Stacey, and Eric cannot wait to join you tomorrow to begin prepping the main grids."

"So, we're moments away from proving this whole idea was worth it?" Maria Elena asked.

"At least to power the station," Flannery said. "After that, we have to prove that we can get energy to the shore."

Maria Elena couldn't take her eyes from the dent in the sand at the ocean bottom. She could still see the submersible after Donnie and Jason were left inside it, everyone unable to reach them.

"Okay, you are clear," Flannery said. "Pull safety pins. Grid is active so we should receive power as soon as they're spinning."

As a tear fell from her eye, Maria Elena took her gaze off the dented ocean floor, and turned to the closest turbine.

"For Donnie and Jason," she said.

The radio was silent for a moment, then Flannery joined in. "For Donnie and Jason."

Maria Elena extended the mechanical claws, reaching for the safety pin at the base of the turbine shell.

"For Donnie and Jason," Cameron radioed.

Maria Elena clenched the safety pin with the claw.

"For Donnie and Jason," Cody said.

She pulled the pin, placing it in the side holder on the concrete base. The turbine started to rise, pushed by the momentum of the ocean current.

"For Donnie and Jason," Karina said.

The turbine rose, then the safety harness tightened, keeping it grounded to the concrete base. Even though it only rose a few meters, to Maria Elena, it looked like a kite soaring into the sky.

"For Donnie and Jason," Yuki radioed.

The lights of the *Anaximander* appeared from the other side on Grid A. Juana piloted the submersible to the edge and pulled her first safety pin. Another turbine rose from the ocean floor. Maria Elena released another. The field of turbines erupted to life as they freed more, blades spinning from the perpetual pressure of the deep ocean current. Juana remained silent, her usual method of dealing with sadness.

Lights within the station turned on. Floodlights outside the station lit up. The *Thales* came into view, the massive, silvery station looking like a sunken spaceship. More turbines floated up, powering what would be their new home for six months until their first rotation ended, and they rotated with the second team, returning again from shore to station.

Maria Elena caught sight of the *Thales* logo where she helped place the shell well over a year ago. Another tear fell. Once they'd pulled the turbines needed to power the station, the two sisters kept their submersibles floating for a second, soaking up the moment as the station came to life.

"God damn, it's beautiful," Maria Elena radioed.

The radio remained quiet, her sister floating in the other submersible, her floodlights shining on the spinning turbines. The station floodlights illuminated the thousands more they would have to activate in the days to come.

But for now, the *Thales* had come to life.

"For Donnie and Jason," Juana radioed.

Maria Elena couldn't help the tears now.

"Congratulations, team," Flannery said. "We are now an operational station. *Archimedes, Anaximander*, come on in for a recharge. We've got a long road ahead, but we also have a lot to celebrate."

Maria Elena passed the dented ocean surface once more on her way in, navigating by the inactive main grids on her way to the loading station. She knew that Donnie and Jason were looking down at them, celebrating. What's more, she knew she would forever treasure that moment, and do everything she could to finish their mission and change how to power the world.

ABOUT THE AUTHOR

Thomas A. Fowler is the author of nerdy things; this is mostly science-fiction. He is an award-winning author with short stories in multiple anthologies, and several non-fiction books helping authors either with writing prompts or marketing. But his love for sci-fi started as a kid always calls him back.

OTHER WORKS BY THOMAS A. FOWLER

THE THALES

The continuation of the characters in *Days to Launch*, the Rising Current Trilogy beings with *The Thales*. If you found yourself wondering what exactly happened to Donnie and Jason, and get to know the new recruits more, it's all available in the novel. A crew of nine descend to the bottom of the Pacific Ocean to harness the power of the deep ocean current to save a failing west coast. However, as disaster looms at every turn, the crew finds their trust in one another failing and the Pacific an ever-increasing threat. But if they can succeed, they could harness the ocean and power the world.

CRASH PHILOSOPHY: FIRST COLLISION

Choose your character. Choose your setting. Choose your journey. A portal has been opened. A portal leading to an expanding universe where science fiction collides with reality, where the future includes a myriad of characters, and each story is as odd as the last. In this anthology, you're given the power to choose where you'll go and who you'll take with you! With this first collision, you can choose between five characters and settings to create twenty-five fictional possibilities.

With stories from authors who write in wildly different genres, each story gives you a different experience. The only question you have to ask is, "How will you crash?"

First Collision characters let you select from an Alien, Clown, Imaginary Friend, Kaiju, and a Robot Assassin. Settings to place them in are an Apocalyptic Wasteland, Evil Laboratory, Human Mind, the Ocean, and the Triassic.

Featuring stories by Scott Beckman, J.M. Butler, J.A. Campbell, Mike Cervantes, Beverly Coutts, Heather Cowley, Thomas A. Fowler, E. Godhand, C.L. Kagmi, Carolyn Kay, Kimberly Kennedy, Jason Kent, A.L. Kessler, Aylâ Larsen, Jennifer Ogden, M.M. Ralph and T.J. Valour.

CRASH PHILOSOPHY: SECOND COLLISION

The portal has expanded to bring 24 new fictional possibilities from 15 authors! With the introduction of a Dinosaur and Psycho Killer as characters, you can place them, and the five previously introduced oddities, in seven different settings. Now, you can take your characters to Space or an Alternate Future. Reenter the crash portal to choose any character or setting combination for a new story pairing. With combinations from authors who write in wildly different genres, each story gives you a different experience. The only question you have to ask is, "How will you crash?"

Featuring stories by Mike Cervantes, Heather Cowley, Jason Henry Evans, Thomas A. Fowler, H.L. Huner, E. Godhand, Kimberly Keane, Melissa Koons, Aylâ Larsen, David Munson, Jennifer Ogden, M.M. Ralph, T.J. Valour and Rob Walker.

PORCELAIN PROMPTS

We all want to write, but finding the time is difficult. There is, however, a time we're all guaranteed: hence *Porcelain Prompts*. With 20 writing prompts and 5 articles, each volume is centered around a writing theme such as Creating Characters or Outlining Your Novel or Conflict & Resolution. When you sit down for a visit on the porcelain throne, plop a little writing into your life. With more volumes coming out all the time, enjoy this award-winning series from authors Thomas A. Fowler and Melissa Koons.

SHATTER YOUR IMAGE

In our lives, people tell us who we should be. We gain the notion we could be happier by trying to be someone else. But we don't have to be perfect for the world, we just have to be ourselves.

Shatter Your Image is an anthology from writers telling stories through fiction and poetry. Stories of being proud of who we truly are, that tragedy and dark moments brought us to a light we didn't think possible. Stories of accepting what some call flaws as cause for celebration. Stories that invite us all to stop changing for others, shatter our image and realize our beauty.

All proceeds from this anthology benefit Realize Your Beauty, a non-profit that promotes positive body image to children & adolescents by way of theatre arts.

THE WRITER'S CONQUEST: ESTABLISH A BRAND

Marketing is hard. You want to focus on your writing and you should. That's why The *Writer's Conquest: Establish Your Brand* exists: to allow you to write first and market second. If the terms "target demographics," "website responsive design," and "organic S.E.O." sound like a foreign language to you, read this book and bring the ad agency experience to your author platform. Beginning with research, you'll learn what goes into brand strategy and finish with an executable marketing plan.

With 35 exercises to walk you through the process, *The Writer's Conquest* is equal parts learning and doing. Whether you are an established author looking to refine your approach, or an aspiring writer gearing up to enter the industry, *The Writer's Conquest* takes marketing step-by-step to sell your books and your brand.